Rel

CLAIRE KENT

PROLOGUE

Hall had never been uncomfortable around sex.

He'd lost his virginity when he was twelve years old to a prostitute who lived down the block from his grandmother. In the twenty-four years since, he'd had sex with women all over Coalition space—and a few men when he was younger and willing to push his limits. He'd fucked and been fucked so many times that he couldn't even remember all their faces, and he'd never known all their names. He'd experimented with kink of every variety, and nothing had ever embarrassed him.

He'd tried everything except a serious relationship.

He wasn't used to feeling uncomfortable where sex was concerned, which was why his slight self-consciousness as he sat in the throne room of the palace of Evalon was so bizarre. The evening's Court festivities were more elaborate than usual because it was a Feast Day, and evidently that meant those in attendance were particularly frisky.

The Lady Governor hadn't even entered the room yet, but the well-dressed people gathered around the banquet tables that filled the large room were already going at it pretty heavily.

A woman sitting at the nearest table to him had leaned over in her chair and was sucking her partner's cock. Hall watched as her cheeks hollowed out at regular intervals and the man's hips started to buck up into her mouth.

There were lush, exotic fruits in the middle of the tables. Fine red wine—as good as replicated wine could get— had been poured into glasses. And that woman was giving a man a blow job right there at the table.

Hall shook his head and looked away.

He was sitting with the other men who had declared themselves "Potentials" of the Lady Governor of Evalon. She would choose one of them each week to be her sex partner until she finally decided on a lifetime companion. They weren't allowed to touch any other woman until the Lady Governor had first rejected them.

Hall needed to get through at least four of these weekly Feast Days so he could remain inside the palace without rousing suspicion. That meant he needed to be careful not to let himself get chosen tonight. For one thing, he didn't want to spend the week giving erotic pleasure to some vain, spoiled Coalition figurehead.

For another, it would take at least a month for him and Lenna to finish this job.

The payoff in the end would be excellent, assuming they could manage it. About half the work they did was smuggling, and this should be a particularly lucrative job since it was so difficult and involved such a time commitment.

If that meant he'd have to suffer through weeks of this tawdry pretense of sexual freedom, then he would do it.

He'd suffered through long weeks on a prison planet, after all, when he'd stupidly let himself get arrested last year in a kidnapping job that went wrong. Nothing here could break him as much as that prison almost had.

The guy beside him in the Potentials section—some mindless, overblown fortune hunter—was getting aroused. Hall could sense it in the guy's presence although he wasn't about to glance over and check out the man's dick for himself.

Hall had to fight not to roll his eyes.

He'd been to these "Court sessions" on the three evenings since he'd arrived, but those had been much less elaborate since they weren't Feast Days. Tonight was something else entirely, and evidently it would go on for hours.

2

He would have earned every ounce of his profit by the time they were done with this job.

To distract himself from his annoyance, he searched the room, looking for interesting faces. He was surprised when his eyes landed on Lenna in the far corner of the room.

She must be attending tonight as a visitor. Most of the people present were visitors—tourists who stupidly thought this planet and this Court were a wild, pleasurable escape from reality.

It all felt fake to Hall—like too many people here were desperately grappling for something, *anything* that might give their lives meaning.

He didn't have any answers for them, but he was too smart and experienced to look for meaning in *this*.

He met Lenna's eyes and shared a knowing look before he glanced away. He couldn't let anyone see that he knew her. He'd worked with her on jobs on and off for years now, and for the past six months, they'd been working together most of the time. He couldn't ask for a better partner.

She was probably secretly laughing her ass off at him, stuck here in the Potentials section with about thirty other losers. Lenna wasn't known for her sympathy or her soft heart.

As Hall looked away, his eyes landed on a woman he'd never seen before, entering the front of the hall through the door only the most important people used.

She wasn't announced in any way, and she walked quietly to the long table on the dais until she reached the chair that had always been vacant on the end.

She was dressed in a silk gown of a deep wine color that shimmered in the light of the room. Her figure was lush and curvy, but she didn't move like someone who flaunted her sexuality. If anything, she looked shy. As if she'd rather be somewhere else.

That was the reason Hall kept watching her. It felt like they were the only two people in this room who really didn't want to be there.

Once she was seated at the table, he could see her more clearly, and he then realized who she was.

The Lady Governor had a sister who evidently was sickly and didn't attend very many Court events. This must be her.

She wasn't strikingly beautiful like her sister, but there was something compelling about her delicately carved features, her full lips, the subtle glinting of her hair.

She didn't show all of herself at first glance. You had to look carefully. You had to look a long time.

Hall entertained himself by watching her, and he was pleased to see that she didn't enjoy all the uninhibited activities going on around her. She looked away from the couples making out and having sex. She sipped her wine only slowly. She occasionally put her hand in front of her face, like there was a scent in the air she didn't like.

She never said a word, even when a few people leaned over to speak to her. She would just smile briefly or nod.

Hall had no idea what to make of her.

Because he was preoccupied, the time went quickly, and he was surprised when he heard a sudden fanfare played by the horns among the musicians in the far corner.

Like everyone else, his eyes moved to the royal entrance where the Lady Governor was making an appearance.

She wore blue silk today to match her eyes and contrast with her fiery red hair. Hall recognized she was beautiful. He didn't like her though.

She gazed out over the people in this room and particularly the men in the Potentials section as if they were her objects.

They probably were, in her mind.

He'd been told what she would do tonight, so he wasn't surprised when she walked over to his section and started to study each man who was lined up with him. She was going to pick out her weekly partner—who was then eligible to be made permanent if he found particular favor with her.

Hall couldn't imagine anything worse than being the consort of someone like her.

He glanced over toward the lovely, interesting woman he'd been watching before, and he saw that her eyes were on her sister. He couldn't read her expression from this far away.

When the Lady Governor stood before him, he held his breath. He absolutely couldn't be chosen, but she spent a long time eying him up and down.

Hall knew he was attractive to women although he couldn't care less about how he looked except how he could use it to his advantage when he was on a job or wanted to fuck someone. Right now he had to hide a cringe when the Lady Governor reached out to touch his fingers.

He immediately opened an internal connection with her through their touch, reading her feelings of interest and attraction and discreetly turning them around so she felt disinterest instead.

He had to be very careful not to expose his unique gift, so the connection was very slight. But it worked. He saw her expression change, and she dropped her hand and moved on to the next Potential.

Hall let out a breath and glanced over to Lenna, who was clearly amused by his close call.

He then turned his eyes back to the sister. Kyla was her name, he remembered now. Her eyes were still on the Lady Governor. She probably hadn't even glanced at him.

Hall didn't want to look or think about anyone else. He wanted her in a way he couldn't remember wanting anyone before. He didn't even know her. He had no idea why he was responding to her this way.

And she hadn't noticed him at all. She didn't even know he existed.

He might be here on a job, but he'd have quite a bit of downtime over the next few weeks.

He was going to make sure she knew he existed before he left this planet.

ONE

For 496 years the planet of Evalon had been known for pleasure and indulgence.

Ever since Mira, the first Empress of Evalon, had set up her Court, filled it with all the most decadent pleasures in the galaxy, and begun a decade-long search for a consort, the planet's culture and reputation had been established, never to be altered. Even when the tyrannical Coalition started to take over the known universe, swallowing up soft, peaceful Evalon with one halfhearted strike, the planet's character didn't change. The ruler might now be called the Lady Governor rather than Empress, but tradition has always died hard, and the nature of the people and their planet never changed.

At least not in any obvious way.

Evalon was still a prime vacation spot for all the surrounding galaxies, and the Court was still as rich and decadent as it had ever been. No royal acts or declarations had been issued from the throne in a hundred years, but Lady Patrice, the current governor, still dictated the behavior and attitudes of her people.

For everyone except her sister, Kyla.

Kyla hated Court almost as much as she hated the Coalition.

Because of her status as a member of the royal family, she wasn't allowed to leave the palace grounds without an escort, but she got away from her royal duties as often as possible. This meant either taking to her bed or taking a walk.

This afternoon, she'd decided to take a walk, mostly to test out her new boots, which she'd just finished making this morning.

The palace grounds consisted of several hundred square miles, and much of the property was uncultivated woods. Today she hiked through the woods on trails she'd found as a child, all the way to one side of the wall that surrounded the palace grounds.

It was there that she encountered the stranger.

He was big and unshaven, and he reeked of generic, replicated whiskey. She could smell it on him from several feet away. He was apparently on a ramble around the grounds, his walk enlivened by the liquor flask he carried.

He made an unpleasant growling sound when he saw her.

Her heartbeat immediately quickening, she gave him a distant smile and turned away, walking in the opposite direction as quickly as she could, without looking like she was running.

Kyla didn't have a problem with men although she had no interest in sex or typical Evalonian entertainments. But she'd found drunk men often forgot the rules, and a few of those forgot basic human decency. Giving them a wide berth had always worked well for her.

Unfortunately, this particular man was a nastier sort of drunk who didn't appreciate being ignored. He followed her even when she stepped back into the woods.

"Where… you going, pretty lil' thing?" he drawled, the unpleasant smell of him intensifying as he got closer.

Okay. Avoiding wasn't working. Maybe an ice-cold smackdown was what he needed. That strategy usually worked when avoidance wasn't an option.

She straightened her spine and turned around to glare at him coolly. "If you'd like company, you could try the public rooms in the palace, or there is an excellent wine bar in the village. I, however, would rather be alone."

His eyes narrowed, and he stepped even closer, forcing her to back away from him. "You're a stuck-up little bitch, aren't you?" He took another gulp from his flask before adding, "That's okay. I can show you what a real man feels like."

Just great. He was drunk and an asshole and an archaic cliché. Male tourists or visitors occasionally acted like this on Evalon. Evidently, the overt sexuality and fantasy fulfillment made them believe they could take anything they wanted. It was one of the reasons security was so abundant in the palace and grounds, and it was why no one but the guards and palace officials could carry weapons.

There was no one else around at the moment, so Kyla said very calmly, the way she would speak to a spooked animal, "I'm sure there are plenty of other women who want to see what a man you are. It's not my thing though. Try the public rooms. Just remember that, on Evalon, the women get to choose. We have a Lady Governor, remember?"

Despite the female governor and the policy of women choosing their sexual partners, women weren't actually in control on Evalon any more than men were in control on other planets in Coalition space. No one was in control except the Coalition Council, and at least they were equal opportunity dominators. They took over male- and female-centric planets indiscriminately in the multitude of galaxies populated by humans who had spread out from Earth in the past thousand years. The Coalition would have taken over the planets of other species too if they'd encountered any other sentient, reasoning life-forms.

"I've got a lady right here," the man mumbled, taking another swig before he dropped his flask on the ground. "Now, come 'ere, little bitch." He leaned even closer to her.

Kyla had never had any such bad behavior aimed at her before. She wasn't pretty enough to attract much attention in Court sessions, and she preferred to avoid public areas as much as possible otherwise. Because she was so surprised, she froze momentarily. She stared at the man as he reached out for her.

Once she realized he was going to touch her, she pushed him away with both hands. "I don't want you to show me anything. Go away!" She spoke very loudly, knowing that intoxicated men were sometimes startled enough by loud confrontation that they stopped whatever they were doing.

This one didn't stop. He just looked angrier. He grabbed her by her shoulders and pushed her back against a tree. "I like a little fight in my bitches."

She was so stunned and terrified that her throat closed up. Her back hurt from where he'd slammed her against the tree, and now his face was leaning in toward her, like he would kiss her.

She was not about to get kissed by this man. She might not be able to scream through the knot in her throat, but she could move. She shoved him away again.

She wasn't strong enough to push him far, but she got enough space between their bodies for her to get her leg up. She kneed him hard in the groin, and then she ran when he doubled over in pain.

She was sweating and chilled at the same time, and she could barely breathe as she broke out of the woods again. The drunk man was actually chasing her. His mind must be so clouded by alcohol and anger that he wasn't thinking clearly. Security drones circled the perimeter of the wall at regular intervals. Once she was spotted by one of those, the palace guards would come to help her.

She stumbled on a dip in the ground, and the man caught up to her before she righted herself, pulling her onto the ground.

Acting purely on instinct, she rolled over and kicked out at him with both legs, as hard as she could, aiming for his knees.

His legs buckled as he roared in pain, and he fell down to the ground beside her.

She heard a drone whizz by and knew help would be coming soon.

Her mind couldn't even process what had happened, what was happening even now. But she knew she wasn't going to let this man touch her.

She didn't let men she knew and liked touch her. She certainly wasn't going to let this disgusting, violent stranger.

~

Hall strode quickly through the woods on a trail he'd found the other day. He was on his way to meet Lenna, which meant he needed to get out of the palace grounds without anyone seeing him.

It wasn't as easy as one would think.

Yesterday he'd found a way though, and he was glad to be getting away—even if just for a short time. He was starting to feel claustrophobic in the palace, trapped by perfume and mirrors and lounging bodies. He hadn't even been able to distract himself with his interest in Kyla, the Lady Governor's sister, since he'd only seen her a few times at Court, and he'd never encountered her alone.

As much as he hated to give up, he was resigning himself to never getting to know her.

He'd reached the edge of the woods and was starting toward the far corner of the wall, where he'd found a way to get over it unseen, when he heard someone cry out.

It sounded like a woman. Like she was in trouble.

Hall wasn't a hero. He'd spent most of his life taking care of himself, trying to save up enough money to live comfortably, to gain financial freedom so he wouldn't have to rely on anyone else. But he wasn't heartless enough to walk away when someone was calling out for help. He turned around and headed toward the voice.

He kept to the edge of the woods so he wouldn't be seen. If the palace officials or guards found out he was trying to get out of the palace, his entire job would be blown. But through the tree branches he saw a man chasing after a woman and pulling her down onto the ground.

Hall jumped forward, rushing to help her.

It was just instinct. If someone was getting raped or assaulted, you helped if you could. At least he still did— especially after those weeks he'd spent in prison, where he hadn't been able to do anything while all manner of cruelty happened around him.

He pulled to a stop when the woman kicked the man's knees out. That was a very good move, bringing down someone much bigger and stronger than she was. This woman fought hard. You never knew how someone would react to being attacked. Freezing was just as natural an instinct as fight or flight—for both men and women—and that instinct had nothing to do with size or strength.

He started moving again, deciding he'd still make sure the man was down for good, but then he saw a couple of the uniformed palace guards approaching with their swords drawn.

The woman was obviously safe now, so Hall stepped back into the shelter of the woods, watching as the guards came over and assisted the woman to her feet.

She was dirty but uninjured, while the man was writhing on the ground in pain.

It was only then that Hall realized the woman was Kyla.

He was relieved she was unharmed, and he was very impressed with her ability to defend herself. But he'd missed his chance to rescue her, to be the hero for her, which was really too bad.

It was like fate had determined that he would never get the chance to know her.

He was tempted to linger, to make sure she was all right and find an opportunity to talk to her, but his brain told him not to. He needed to get into the village so he could meet with Lenna, and the guards would be suspicious if he tried to hang around Kyla.

She was off-limits to him, and it looked like she always would be.

He was slightly shaky from the release of adrenalin from his interrupted charge to the rescue, but he shook it off and turned around.

The job was always the most important thing. He couldn't afford to let anything else become a priority in his life—not if he was ever going to reach a point where he finally felt free.

~

When the palace guards helped her to her feet, Kyla was trembling so hard she could barely stand.

She recognized both guards, and she knew one of them by name.

Harley scanned her in concern. "Are you all right, Lady Kyla?"

"Yes." She cleared her throat when her voice broke, and she wrapped her arms around her belly. "But this man needs to be escorted off-world. He obviously can't follow the rules."

The guards clearly understood what had happened, and they didn't hesitate to haul the drunken man up, despite his loud protests, and put him in metal cuffs.

"Do you need help getting back to your room, Lady Kyla?" Harley asked. He was short, stocky, and normally quiet. His eyes were always kind.

"No, thank you. I'm a little shaky, so I think I'll just walk it off."

She mostly wanted to be alone. Adrenalin was still coursing through her, and her panic had halted so quickly that she couldn't physically process it.

Her stomach churned queasily, and she felt a dull throbbing begin behind her right eye.

She needed to calm down quickly or she would get a migraine. She got them often, and they always knocked her out.

When the guards had disappeared with the grumbling would-be rapist, Kyla tried to take deep breaths and pull herself together. She needed to be where she felt safe, and there were only two places in the world where she felt that way. One was in her room. That was too far away though, so she headed to the other one.

She reached the tree in just a minute, and she started to climb it. She had to move slowly since she was still trembling from her earlier encounter.

For thirteen years, ever since she'd found this tree at ten years old, she'd sat on a big, flat branch shaped like a seat and looked out over the wall, watching the world go by beneath her.

It was a beautiful day, with warm air, vivid blue sky, and both moons full and visible, hovering just beneath the sun. All the days here were mostly the same, since they were created by the sophisticated habitation generator, and Kyla was barely conscious of the beauty of her surroundings.

She could still smell that man's breath. She kept imagining what would have happened if she hadn't gotten away from him. In an attempt to feel better, she reached for the binoculars she kept hidden in a little hole in the tree.

The gardens of Evalon used to extend all the way around the village and much farther, but they'd been forced to reduce the size of habitable land on the planet a hundred years ago in compliance with Coalition policies about the limits of personal property. Now the lush and lovely landscape—the white turrets of the palace buildings, fragrant orchards, and vast stretches of lavender fields—was much smaller than it used to be.

Kyla didn't focus her binoculars on the palace or grounds though. She focused them on the only road from the palace.

Since it was still early, a lot of the townspeople were still on their way to work in the specialty shops that filled the village. Since motorized vehicles weren't allowed in the village or palace grounds, except on official business, tourists and locals either walked or were carried in hired litters. The village scene was as it usually was except for the two guards who were walking that terrible man to the public launch port and docking station on the outskirts of town.

Kyla kept watching them until they were out of sight, blocked by other buildings. She took comfort in the fact that the man would never be allowed to come back to Evalon.

Out of habit she refocused her lenses on the terrace of an outdoor café that was built high so it would overlook the palace grounds. It was popular with tourists who couldn't afford to rent rooms in the palace, and she often saw interesting people there. As she scanned over a few families and couples, she wondered what it would be like to eat at the café, to wander the village, to vacation to another planet.

To do anything on her own, without the palace guards as escort.

She never had, and she probably never would. Her life had been dictated by her birthright, just as surely as her sister's had.

Patrice was born to be the Lady Governor, the head of a decadent Court, the arbiter of taste and culture. She was born to launch a far-ranging search for a consort, something she'd begun more than five years ago now.

Kyla, on the other hand, was born to wilt away in the shadows of the palace, as the backup in case Patrice died before giving birth to a daughter, unable to do anything for herself until Patrice gave birth to an heir.

Kyla glanced over the other tables in the café, deciding to put the binoculars down and head back. She still felt a familiar faint throbbing behind her right eye that warned her a migraine might be coming on. The only way to dull the pain was with an injection she kept in her room. She needed to get back before the migraine came on strong. She was feeling more like herself now anyway, the adrenalin from before starting to dissipate. She gave the café one last sweep, deciding she was steady enough to walk back now, when she recognized a familiar face at the corner table.

He was one of the current Potentials.

There were always twenty or thirty Potentials in Court at any time, and they blended together in Kyla's mind in a blur of broad shoulders, handsome faces, and fine clothes. The only reason Kyla recognized this man was because he'd been almost chosen as Patrice's partner for the past two weeks.

He shouldn't be at the café. Potentials weren't allowed to leave the palace grounds or be in the company of a woman once they'd declared themselves—not until Patrice had rejected them.

This dark-haired man shouldn't be here. It was against the law. Kyla straightened up and focused on his face, unconsciously appreciating the well-chiseled features and charismatic smile. He was incredibly good-looking and had an air of almost unnatural confidence, as if there had never been anything he couldn't claim. He had smiled and flipped his hands in showy resignation when he hadn't been chosen last week.

Patrice had been stupid to choose the blond man for her weekly partner instead of this one. The overblown physique and bland handsomeness of the blond wasn't nearly as compelling as this man.

But what the hell was he doing outside the palace walls?

As Kyla watched, a blond woman approached the table at which he sat. She smiled as she joined him, and they began to speak. The woman was very pretty in a no-nonsense way— in her plain trousers, boots, and jacket—but their conversation didn't look romantic or even personal. It looked like business.

This man was up to trouble. Something was wrong. He should not be having a business conversation with an unknown woman when he was a Potential in the Court of Evalon.

Kyla searched his face but couldn't read anything except interest and faint amusement. There must be more going on in his head that she just couldn't see. She'd spent her life in the shadows while her sister had gotten all the attention. Kyla knew how to read people. She didn't understand why she couldn't read this man.

The conversation only lasted three or four minutes, and then the man got up to leave. It was very strange. Maybe they'd just met up to trade information.

But what kind of information?

Instead of heading toward the closest palace gates, the man started toward the wall. Kyla immediately knew where he was going.

He wasn't supposed to be outside the walls at all, and there was only one way to get back in without confronting the well-trained guards.

Kyla had found it as a kid and had snuck outside the wall a few times until her punishments after being caught had become painful enough to keep her inside. She had no idea how this man had found it so quickly.

The woods grew right up to the wall in one corner, and vines had grown up all over the stones. In the shade from the trees, one could time it right between the sweeps of the security drones and use the vines to climb up and over the wall.

She headed to the spot and sat down on a bench nearby. She had no idea why she was doing this except she'd felt helpless when that man had attacked her earlier, and now she wanted to do something to make herself feel stronger. She wanted to confront something—or someone.

She only had to wait five minutes before the good-looking, dark-haired man climbed over the wall with a strength and agility that was very impressive.

When he saw her on the bench, she caught a brief flash of surprise that he quickly hid.

This man was definitely a cool customer.

"Good morning," he said with a broad smile that probably left most women breathless. Up close, she could see that he had remarkably vivid green eyes.

"What are you doing?" she asked, standing up and stepping toward him.

"Exploring."

"You're a Potential. You're not allowed to explore."

He sighed and gave her another smile, this one adorably sheepish. "Are you going to tell your sister?"

She was surprised he knew who she was. Most people didn't even notice her. "I don't know," she admitted, telling him the truth.

His smile warmed. "I'll convince you as we walk back to the palace."

The throbbing behind her eye had intensified in the past few minutes as she'd been distracted by this man's behavior. But she felt it now again, so strongly she covered her eye with her hand, trying to will the migraine back until she returned to her room.

"What's wrong?" the man asked, his expression changing.

"Nothing." She lowered her hand.

He didn't look convinced. "Did something happen?"

It was like he knew what had happened to her earlier—or almost happened to her—but there was no way that was possible. "Of course not."

"Let's head back to the palace."

"I didn't invite you to walk with me."

"Then I'll walk behind you. We're heading in the same direction, after all."

She felt a tug of attraction and appreciation, despite her best efforts to hold this man at a suspicious distance. He must be used to charming the pants off any woman he encountered, but she wasn't going to be one of those women.

She frowned at him and turned around, starting back to the shortest trail that led to the palace. As promised, he walked behind her, but she was intensely aware of his presence.

It felt like his eyes were running up and down her body.

She was wearing her normal outfit—a long tunic, riding trousers, and the new boots she'd just completed—but she suddenly wished she was dressed more attractively. It was such an unusual feeling for her that she decided her close encounter earlier had completely rattled her.

"I wondered if you could talk," the man said after a minute of silence.

She tensed. "What do you mean?"

"Well, I've been here two weeks, and I've only seen you at Court three times. You've never said a word any of those times."

She felt a shiver of self-consciousness at the knowledge that he'd noticed her so acutely. She covered her right eye with her palm again as she walked. The migraine was coming on quickly. It was going to be full-blown before she reached the palace. She'd been a fool not to head back as soon as she'd noticed the first sign. "How do you know I haven't said a word?"

"Because I've watched you."

"Not the whole time."

"No, but enough to notice if you'd spoken to anyone. You haven't. I found it very strange."

She was getting tired of his voice coming from behind her, so she paused until he fell in stride with her. "It's not strange. Court is about Lady Patrice. It's not about me."

"Maybe. But other women seem to have a good time. Why not you?"

"It's not my thing."

"Pleasure isn't your thing?"

"Court is not what I enjoy. All that sex and overindulgence."

"Sex isn't your thing?"

She felt her cheeks warming for no good reason. She wasn't remotely embarrassed to talk about sex. It had been part of her world and culture since she was twelve years old and she'd first made her presence at Court. She had no idea why she'd be blushing at this man's blunt question. "No," she told him, feeling another shiver of fear as she felt the migraine intensifying. "It's all... empty."

"So you stopped having sex entirely?"

She frowned. "I never started. The whole thing makes me... sick. It's my sister's thing. Not mine."

The man started to say something in reply, but he broke off when Kyla stopped abruptly, pressing into her eye with the heel of her hand. "Do you have a headache or something?" he asked in a different tone.

She swallowed hard. "Migraine."

"You have medicine for it?"

"A shot in my room. It's the only thing that works. I've gotten these for years."

She felt the blood run out of her face as a wave of dizziness overcame her. It was very bad now, and she still had more than a mile to walk. It was brutally unjust of the universe to have her almost assaulted and then get a migraine in the same day.

The man stood quietly beside her as she took a few deep breathes. When she was able to lower her hand, he asked softly, "Are you okay?"

She managed to nod. "I just need to get back."

"Okay."

They walked in silence for a few minutes until Kyla started to stumble as her eyes blurred over in pain. Pretty soon she was going to start vomiting. She always did when the migraines hit her this hard.

The man reached out to put a supportive arm around her, the only thing that kept her from falling.

"You're not allowed to touch me," she mumbled.

"This is an emergency. I won't tell if you don't."

She leaned on him because she couldn't help it, and it was strangely relieving to have his warm, strong body for support. He wasn't as big as a lot of men in Court, but he was hard and strong and could easily hold her up.

Maybe it was just the contrast to how that other man had felt earlier, but she really liked how this one felt.

She wouldn't have been able to keep walking if he hadn't been supporting her, but soon the pain and nausea intensified so much her legs just wouldn't hold her weight. She drooped against him, and he held her up with both arms.

"Should I go get help?" he murmured.

"No. I can make it. Just give me a minute."

She tried to breathe, vaguely conscious of the fact that one of his hands was gently rubbing her back. It was entirely inappropriate. No man was allowed to touch her without permission, and this one wasn't allowed to touch anyone at all until Patrice rejected him as a Potential. But she didn't have the will to stop him. She didn't even want to.

His hand slowly slid higher on her back until it was touching the bare skin at the nape of her neck.

She shivered as he gently massaged her there. She was dazed from the pain, but she was faintly conscious of a strange inner tug, somehow connected to his touch.

Immediately following it, she was washed with a deep wave of pleasure and relief.

The migraine wasn't gone, but it was better. She collapsed more fully against his weight as the relief almost knocked her out. "What did you do?" she gasped.

"Nothing. Just massaged your neck. I know I'm not supposed to, but I thought it would help." One of his arms was wrapped around her, holding her up, and the other was rubbing her back through the fabric of her top.

"Do it again," she panted, clinging to his arms and dazed from the sudden relief from pain.

He moved his hand back up to her neck and massaged the muscles there. It felt nice, relaxing, and then she felt that little inner tug again—almost imperceptible this time. The pleasure from it wafted over her, filling her body so deeply that she gasped helplessly.

He held her against him for another minute until he finally cleared his throat and asked, "Do you think you can walk now?" His body had tightened, and he gently straightened her up so she wasn't draped against him anymore.

She blinked, barely able to think but feeling so much better she didn't even care. "Yeah. Yeah. Sorry."

"Don't be sorry. I've never had a migraine, but they seem terrible."

"They are." She was still aware of the painful throbbing, but it was bearable now, so she made herself start walking. She shook her head slightly, trying to clear her mind. "What just happened?" she asked after a minute.

"What do you mean?" His expression was bland, completely innocent.

"It felt like you did something."

"I told you. Just massaged your neck. I thought it might help."

She narrowed her eyes. "It felt like more than that."

He gave a shrug and a little smile. "While I'd like to possess healing powers, I'm afraid they're beyond me. Migraines make you spacey. You probably imagined it."

"Maybe." She wasn't convinced, but she couldn't make her mind work enough to figure it out.

"Let's get you back so you can get your medicine."

She didn't talk as they walked back. She was now able to mostly support herself, and the man just kept his hand on the small of her back, as assistance if she needed it. She liked how it felt there. She'd liked how it felt when he touched her, when she'd leaned on him.

She'd never felt that way before, and she had no idea where it was coming from now.

And then there had been that strange tug, one that felt like something even more.

She definitely needed to get back to her room and return to her senses.

They made it to the edge of the woods—not far from the back entrance—and then they stopped in unison, both of them obviously realizing the same thing.

"We'll have to go in separately," she said. "We can't be seen talking."

"I know. Are you going to be okay?" His eyes were scanning her face, and it felt like he could see deep inside her, all the way to her core. "You've had a hard day."

He couldn't have known how hard it really had been.

"Yes." The migraine was starting to intensify again. The relief she'd felt at his touch obviously couldn't last. She wondered who in the universe this man was. "What's your name?"

"Hall."

"Oh. I'm Kyla."

"I know who you are."

The words sounded strangely significant. They made her shiver and flush, and then the throbbing of the migraine made her dizzy. She reached out to cling to his shirt when her knees almost buckled.

He gently brushed her hair before he dropped his hand, as if he'd remembered he shouldn't be touching her.

"What did you do to me?" she asked, still trying to figure out what had happened earlier.

"Nothing."

"It was something."

"It was just your imagination."

"It wasn't."

"You're in no shape to argue," he said, stepping back slightly from her.

That was true. She needed to lie down, give herself a shot. "What were you doing outside the walls?"

"Taking a walk. I don't like to be penned up, even in a palace." He smiled and met her eyes.

The last bit was true. She could see it in his expression. But the rest of what he'd said was a lie. She knew he was hiding something, lying to her.

She couldn't trust him. He was dangerous. And she definitely shouldn't be clinging to him this way.

She let her hands fall to her sides. "I'll go in first. You wait a few minutes."

He nodded. "Feel better."

Again there seemed to be more going on in his voice and expression than she could figure out, but she just didn't have the strength to stay and unravel it. "Good-bye, Hall," she mumbled, limping out of the shade of the trees and toward the back entrance of the palace.

There was just one guard there, and he was used to her going out and taking walks. He wouldn't suspect she'd been talking to someone she shouldn't be, touching someone who wasn't allowed to touch her.

She was so distracted by Hall that she'd almost forgotten her near trauma earlier. And that was troubling in a different way. No man should be able to make her forget something like that, even for a few moments.

It would be best for her to avoid Hall in the future, but she couldn't help but wonder when she would see him again.

~

Hall watched Kyla cross the courtyard and then disappear into the palace through the small door.

His head was still whirling, filled with her—her pain, her relief, and a fresh kind of sweetness he hadn't tasted in a really long time.

He'd been stupid to open a channel with her. Even with her migraine, she'd recognized that he'd done something. It was dangerous. He didn't know her well enough to trust her, and there had been no real need to expose himself to her like that.

For decades now, the Coalition had been rounding up Readers, using the gifts of those who were willing, and then killing or imprisoning the others. Readers could tap into other people's minds, and that was a skill too powerful for the Coalition to ignore.

But Hall could do more than that. His mother and grandmother and great-grandmother had all been Readers, but the gift had transformed into something else in him. He could do more than read what another was feeling. He could turn it around—make them feel something different.

The Coalition would never allow him to exist if they knew.

Which was why it was even more important for him not to do something as foolish as use his gift on Kyla when it wasn't a life-or-death situation. She'd been in so much pain. He'd wanted to make it better.

And, honestly, he'd wanted to taste her ever since he'd first seen her, sitting in the midst of a wild, sensuous Court, completely untouched by it.

Now he couldn't wait to taste her again.

TWO

The migraine drug always knocked her out, so Kyla slept all afternoon.

It wasn't all that unusual. She had migraines at least a few times a month, and sometimes she pretended to have one so she wouldn't be dragged into the superficial political or diplomatic issues her sister spent her days on—which were nearly all a waste of time and yet managed to take up a ridiculously long amount of time.

Better to spend the day in her room than to be forced to sit, bored and useless, listening to other people talk.

By sunset the drug had mostly worn off, and Kyla had to decide whether to go down to Court for the night.

It was the last day of the week, Feast Day, which meant the most indulgent and debauched Court session of the week. Patrice would choose her new weekly partner, and everyone else would spend all night eating, feasting, and debauching themselves.

Patrice was usually pretty tolerant about Kyla bowing out, but this was the one evening of the week she was expected to make an appearance.

Her migraine was gone. She felt groggy and tired but not in pain anymore. And Hall would be down there tonight. She wanted to keep her eye on him. He might be chosen for Patrice's partner this week.

For no good reason that idea bothered Kyla. Probably because she was so suspicious of Hall. She didn't trust him around Patrice, and she didn't like the idea of him devoting the entire week to pleasing her.

Determined to attend, if only to watch him, Kyla bathed quickly and then brushed her hair as she decided what to wear.

When there was a tap on the private door at the back of her suite, Kyla knew who it was.

"Come in, Patrice."

Her sister stepped into the room, looking as radiant as ever and smiling at her sister. "You look like you feel better. I was just coming in to check on you."

"Yes, I feel better."

"The guards told me about what happened earlier—with that man."

"Oh. Yes. Nothing happened, and he's been banished."

"Good. I told them to beef up security anyway. We can't have tourists here who act that way."

"Most of them don't."

"As long as you're okay."

"I'm fine."

"So you're going down to Court."

"Yes. I guess so."

"Good. I was afraid you'd want to sit it out tonight, and you won't want to miss what the chef has been preparing for us."

The food was always scrumptious—every night of the week and even more so on the last day of the week.

This evening, Patrice wore flowing silk robes of crimson and indigo, her flaming red hair brushed smooth and flowing in a shiny fall down her back. She was gorgeous, with her vivid blue eyes and fair skin and long, slim build. When she was younger, Kyla had been intensely jealous of her sister's looks. Now she was just resigned.

Where Patrice burned like a magnificent fire, Kyla faded into the background. She had sandy hair that sometimes looked blond and sometimes reddish, but mostly just plain old light brown. Her eyes were a boring blue gray, and her body soft and curvy—despite the amount of walking she did—instead of sleek and lithe. She would never look like Patrice, and it was really just as well since she preferred not to get that kind of attention.

"What are you going to wear?"

"I don't know yet." Kyla walked over to her wardrobe and stared at the piles of evening gowns. Patrice might have inherited the entire wealth, property, and title of their family, but she was generous and constantly supplied her sister with new clothes. Usually Kyla just grabbed the first thing she saw, but today she scanned over the options, wondering what would look best on her.

"You should wear that rust-colored silk. You look gorgeous in it." Patrice came over to stand beside her, reaching out for a long gown that draped over one shoulder, cinched with a sash at the waist, and then slid slinkily down the legs. The fabric was thick and lush and shimmered with a subtle smolder, like a dying fire.

Kyla couldn't remember the last time she'd worn the gown, but if Patrice said it was good, then it was. "Okay. Thanks. I will."

While she slipped on the clothes, Patrice watched her thoughtfully. "Please say you'll choose a partner today."

In the Court of Evalon, after Patrice made her choice for the week, the ladies always chose their partners. Sometimes just for the evening, sometimes for the week like their Lady

Governor, and sometimes for a lifetime if they happened on one they really liked.

"It's not for me," Kyla murmured softly, trying to sound gentle and not impatient. She was tired of having this conversation with her sister.

"But it's getting to be embarrassing. I'm the Empress, and my own sister refuses to follow our old customs. People will think something is wrong with you."

"I don't care what they think."

"But *I* care. What you do reflects on me. You know that's true."

Of course it was. But Kyla couldn't imagine how having a celibate sister could impact her sister in any serious way. Everyone loved Patrice. "I'll think about it," she said at last, mostly to end the topic of conversation. "And by the way, you need to be careful about calling yourself the Empress."

"I am the Empress." Patrice squared her shoulders and straightened her spine. She was regal, authoritative, breathtaking.

"I know—in spirit. But by the letter of Coalition law, the Empress doesn't exist anymore. And they're not going to like it if news gets back to them that you're defying them. They've mostly left of us alone since they don't think we're a threat, but they're going to have more of a presence here if they think there's a rebellion brewing."

"There's no rebellion brewing. But just because they won't let me be called by my rightful title doesn't mean that's not who I am."

Kyla gave up on tying her sash and turned toward her sister. "Seriously. It's dangerous. If the Coalition Council finds out, the best-case scenario would be they post soldiers and officials here—even in Court. Just think what that would do to our tourism earnings. People come here to forget about the

Coalition. We can't have them breathing down our necks. Promise me you won't call yourself the Empress with anyone but me."

Patrice laughed and leaned over to kiss Kyla's cheek, as blithely beautiful as ever. "You're so cute, worrying like that. You always were unnaturally serious." She tied Kyla's hanging sash and then patted her on the hip. "There. You look beautiful. Now go downstairs and try to have fun. Find yourself a man."

Kyla released a long breath as she stared at herself in the mirror. Her sister was hopeless. She could only pray they stayed off Coalition radar. She did look nice though, since the color of the gown brought out the reddish glints of her hair and made her eyes look bluer. She wasn't planning to find a man though.

She wondered if Patrice would choose Hall tonight.

~

When she entered the throne room twenty minutes later, the festivities were in full swing.

The banquet was laid out on the table—the best of meats, breads, and exotic fruits available to them through their sophisticated replicators, as well as an array of decadent desserts. The wine had been served for more than an hour now, so people were laughing and talking riotously. The musicians in the far corner were playing traditional Evalonian melodies on the lute, harp, and horns. The dancers would come out later.

It was a feast for all five senses, but Kyla was immediately hit with the perfume—from far too many Court ladies gathered together in one enclosed space.

The scent slammed into her like a wave, making her head throb with a dull ache. Not a migraine, fortunately. Just her normal Court headache.

She'd just arrived, but she could already tell it was going to be a long night.

She went to take her seat on the far end of the royal table on the dais. Because of her relationship with Patrice, she should have sat near the center, but she'd given that seat up long ago. She didn't like to be the center of attention, and at the end she could stay mostly out of sight. The rest of the attenders and visitors were spread out among round tables that filled the large room, with a section roped off on the right side for the Potentials.

As soon as she sat down, Kyla's eyes moved automatically to the Potentials section. She scanned the faces quickly until her gaze landed on Hall.

He was watching her. He looked handsome and sophisticated in silver and charcoal silk and velvet, and he appeared relaxed and confident, unlike the tense excitement she could read in the auras of the other Potentials.

When he noticed her looking at him, the corner of his mouth twitched up, and he gave her a very slight wink.

She looked away quickly, embarrassed for no good reason and afraid someone would see.

She shouldn't be looking at Potentials, and they definitely shouldn't be looking at her.

After a few minutes the horns interrupted the chatter of the room with a fanfare, causing everyone to fall into silence. Then Patrice entered, smiling graciously and giving a practiced flutter of her hands when the room burst into applause.

It happened every night, and the room was particularly enthusiastic this evening, given the quality of food and wine being served.

The first thing Patrice did on Feast Days was choose her partner. The room quieted quickly as she walked over to the section of Potentials.

Kyla found herself holding her breath as her sister walked from seat to seat, making a great show of studying each man and occasionally asking them questions.

She paused in front of Hall and said something, but the question was too soft for Kyla to hear. She closed her fingers into a fist, wondering why it mattered so much to her. It didn't matter if Patrice took Hall as her man for the week. She'd toss him aside afterward, the way she did every other man.

Patrice spent a long time in front of Hall. She even reached out to touch his hand. Kyla shuddered, her stomach churning.

She needed to resign herself to her sister having Hall. She got everything else she wanted. Nothing had ever been Kyla's, and it was fine. It was the way of the world—*every* world. You just couldn't change the turnings of the universe, and those turnings had made Kyla a younger sister.

She had nothing to complain about. Her life was better than most. She'd always been comfortable, never been deprived or hurt. To want any more was silly and selfish.

When her sister moved on, she let out her breath. It wasn't decided yet, but at least Patrice hadn't chosen Hall immediately. She might come back for him though.

Kyla watched and waited, her eyes shifting briefly back to Hall, trying to read his expression. His eyes met hers again, but this time he looked curious, as if he was trying to figure something out.

Hopefully, he wasn't trying to figure *her* out. She had no idea what he might see if he looked too closely.

When Patrice had gotten to the end of the row— studying all twenty-four of the current Potentials—she extended her hand and laid her fingers on the forehead of a very handsome man with thick brown hair and sexily drooping eyes. He'd just arrived yesterday. This was his first week, and he was already chosen.

Kyla should have known to expect it. Patrice always had liked men like that. Hall was too intelligent for her. Too much was going on under his surface. Patrice had never liked that in a man.

Trying to hide how ridiculously relieved she felt that Hall hadn't been chosen, she looked back toward him. He was watching her again. It was unnerving. What could he possibly hope to see? When he met her eyes, he gave her a little smile, as if he were amused, pleased by something.

What the hell could he be pleased about? He'd been rejected by Patrice again. He wouldn't be a Potential if he hadn't been hoping to be her consort. He should be as disappointed as all the other Potentials rejected this week.

Patrice's choice went up to the throne with her, seated at her right hand at the royal table. Then Patrice waved her arm, and all the other ladies stood up and went to search for their partners.

With the exception of the Potentials, any man in the room was fair game, even those who had come with their lifetime partners. You didn't come to the Court of Evalon unless you were prepared to spend the night with a Court lady.

Kyla didn't move. She never chose a man—except for a few times she'd requested the company of men she knew well, who wouldn't expect any physicality. This evening, she scanned the room, trying to avoid Hall's eyes.

She had no idea why he was still watching her.

In her attempt to avoid his gaze, her eyes focused on a familiar face. Commander Tor. He'd been born on Evalon and trained by the Palace Guard, moving his way up to the top rank at a surprisingly early age. Kyla knew him well. He was a few years older than her, but they'd played together as kids.

She'd always liked him. He'd been off-world for a while, sent on some mission for Patrice. Kyla smiled and got up, walking down off the dais and over to Tor, who was lounging in his chair with a cup of wine.

He was obviously off duty tonight.

There was no particular reason that Kyla wanted to have a partner tonight, but she did.

Tor grinned back at her as she approached and stood up as she extended her hand.

"Do you want to sit with me?" she asked.

"Of course." He had a strong, pleasant face and lovely blue eyes. He was almost a foot taller than her with impressive shoulder breadth. "Just to sit, I assume, unless you've changed your habits in the months I've been gone."

"Just to sit."

He nodded and followed her up to the royal table, taking the seat next to her.

When Kyla glanced over to Hall, he was arching his eyebrows inquisitively, his gaze moving from her to Tor. Kyla suddenly wished she wasn't in his line of sight.

The servers started to walk around with trays of food and carafes of red, white, and blue wine. The couples around her had already started to kiss, to touch, and soon it would go much further.

"How were things off-world?" Kyla asked Tor, trying to distract herself from the setting.

"As it's always been. Cold, rigid, and barren." Tor gave a faint smile. "Too much Coalition and not enough character."

Kyla nodded as his words summarized all her feelings about the Coalition shadow that had now fallen over most of the known universe and changed the lifestyle of all but the most primitive and isolated of planets. "We've managed to hold on to our world here—for the most part."

"Yes." Tor sighed and leaned back in his seat. "Although I'm not sure how long it will last."

"What do you mean?"

"Evalon is flourishing economically, and it only has one Coalition outpost. How long do you think it is before the Council starts to notice?"

"But tourists come because of our traditions and rituals. If we became more in line with the Coalition, they would stop coming."

"Yes, but that kind of logic doesn't always occur to them."

Kyla's eyes scanned the lushly decorated room, filled with all kinds of worldly beauty and indulgences. It was almost too much—an excess of any desire known to humankind—and it made Kyla dizzy as she tried to process it. It felt empty to her, all surface, no depth, but that didn't mean she wanted it wiped out in favor of gray walls and stoic utilitarianism. "Do you really think we're in danger?"

"If we can stay off the radar, we might be all right. But you might advise your sister against claiming any position or history above the Coalition-ordained governor."

Kyla swallowed hard. It was exactly what she'd told Patrice earlier. If Tor, Commander of the Palace Guard and the most strategically savvy man of her acquaintance, had noticed it too, then there was definitely something to be worried about. "I've already told her. She doesn't tend to listen to advice."

Tor's eyes were on the throne now where Patrice was lounging back in a pleased sprawl, her chosen escort kneeling between her legs, caressing her beneath her skirt. "She should start listening," he said.

Kyla's concern temporarily distracted her, but soon the behavior around her became too pronounced to ignore. Patrice set the mood and manner of each evening's Court. Today was obviously more about debauchery than formality since she was letting the man between her legs pleasure her so early in the evening. The people around her followed suit, and soon the room was full of moans of pleasure, pants and grunts, and writhing, tangled bodies.

Her stomach tightened with that familiar sick feeling. She didn't understand the appeal. It was so empty, superficial, over the top. No orgasm was worth descending into that kind of soulless physicality.

She and Tor ate and chatted occasionally for an hour, but it was too loud in the room for real conversation, and the woman beside them—Patrice's friend Breah—was practically screaming her head off as the tourist she'd picked out was tonguing between her legs.

Breah certainly seemed to be enjoying it, but Kyla didn't want some stranger to lick her intimately. She didn't want to make a fool of herself, losing control like that in front of everyone she knew. She didn't want to be flushed and damp with perspiration and clutching at anything she could reach as her body shook and jerked so awkwardly. She didn't want to scream herself hoarse in exaggerated pleasure.

Nothing could really feel that good and be so empty at the same time. Even if it did feel good, it never lasted.

Tomorrow all these women would be tired and sulky and bored. Kyla knew it from long experience.

At least she would wake up feeling the same as she felt today. Like herself.

"You sure I can't tempt you to try something?" Tor asked, leaning over to murmur the question into her ear.

Kyla looked at him in surprise. He was slightly flushed, and a quick look at his crotch proved that he was turned on. It wasn't surprising, given what he was seeing around him.

"No," she said with a smile. "Thank you though. You probably should have accepted a different partner."

"Never." His smile was sincere.

She chuckled and reached over into his lap, finding his hard cock beneath the fabric of his trousers. "I can give you a hand job since you got unlucky in your partner." She'd done it often enough. It was easy and didn't mean anything to her, and she felt kindly toward Tor at the moment.

"Thank you. I'd appreciate it." He gasped when she slid her fingers beneath his waistband and then gasped again as she started to pump him with her hand.

Kyla smiled at him, but she didn't like to meet a man's eyes when she did this, so she glanced away, looking around at the room.

Quite without volition, her eyes landed on Hall. He was sitting unmoved, like the rest of the Potentials, but his gaze was once again focused on her. Now he was frowning slightly.

When their eyes met, she couldn't look away. She kept massaging Tor's cock in a practiced manner—men were much easier than women in this regard—but she kept staring at Hall. She felt another hot flush waft over her and a tightening between her legs that completely surprised her.

Breah was crying out loudly again right next to her, almost sobbing as she worked herself up to yet another orgasm. The man she'd chosen must be good. Next to her, a man had bent a woman over the table and was taking her hard from behind. The woman's face was bright red and her eyes tightly closed, and she was clinging hard to the far edge of the table as he pushed into her.

And Hall was still staring at Kyla.

It shouldn't make her feel this way—like she wanted him to be doing all that to her.

She never felt that way. It was completely unprecedented, completely unnerving.

Tor grunted a few times as she sped up her rhythm, trying to get him off quickly so she could be distracted by something else. But she couldn't seem to turn her eyes away from Hall.

The man was some sort of magician if he was doing this to her. She remembered what it had felt like when he'd massaged her neck, that rush of unexpected pleasure.

She wondered what it would feel like if he touched other parts of her body.

Her pussy was throbbing deeply now, and she was wet between her legs. This wasn't who she was. It wasn't who she wanted to be. She finished Tor off quickly and pulled her hand back to herself.

"Thank you," Tor said, relaxing back with a pleased smile. "You're good at that."

She wasn't sure that was true. Anyone could get an aroused man off with her hand. But Tor was being polite, so she returned the favor. "My pleasure. I'm glad you were my partner tonight. I had a migraine earlier, and I think it's coming back. Would you mind if I slipped away early."

"Of course not. I've got duty first thing tomorrow morning anyway." He picked up her hand and kissed her knuckles, and she gave him a flustered smile before she got up and hurried out of the throne room, giving a brief explanation to the Court director, Malone, as she exited.

Patrice would be angry, but Kyla didn't care. She needed to get out of there. Feel like herself again.

She wasn't one of those silly women led on by superficial touches. And Hall wasn't going to turn her into one.

She was in the hallway, heading toward the royal wing of the palace, when she heard a voice call out to her. Sometimes, when she left early, Patrice would send a guard to call her back into the throne room, but that wasn't who was calling out to her.

Kyla sucked in her breath as she recognized the voice, and she knew who she'd see when she paused and looked over her shoulder.

Hall.

He must have followed her, which was the strangest thing.

"What are you doing out here?" she demanded as he approached. "You'll get in trouble for leaving. Potentials are supposed to stay all night and study up on what pleases Lady Patrice."

Hall looked half-amused, which must be his characteristic expression. "I mastered that lesson after my first evening. From what I can see, pleasing her is not that complicated."

"But still, you're not supposed to leave."

"*You* left. Do you still have a migraine?" His eyes changed from irony to what looked like genuine concern.

She shook her head. "Just a little headache from all the perfume. I was just... tired."

"Were you?" He stepped closer to her, causing her to move backward.

"Yes."

"And that's reason enough to leave on a Feast Day?"

It wasn't—not nearly good enough reason—but Hall wouldn't necessarily know this. "I'm Lady Patrice's sister. I can leave when I want."

"What's the matter?" He was still moving toward her until her back hit the wall of the hallway. He stood very close—far too close. It felt *very* different from when the gross man had her cornered earlier today.

"Nothing's the matter."

"I think something is."

"Well, it's none of your business."

"It feels like my business." His voice was soft, hoarse, very seductive. It made her shiver.

"You're a Potential. Your only business is to find a way to please Lady Patrice. That's written in the law, you know."

He curled up his lips and glanced briefly down the hall, toward the throne room. "That's rather an outdated law, don't you think?"

"We believe in outdated here. You know that. That's why you're not allowed any technology within the village and palace limits. The guards don't even carry mechanized weapons. We like all our old-fashioned customs and rituals."

"You don't."

"What do you mean?"

"You don't participate in the rituals going on in there. You don't like them. It's a kind of silent rebellion, I think."

She stiffened. "It is not."

"I think it is. I've been watching you."

"Well, you shouldn't be watching me. You should be watching Lady Patrice."

"You're more interesting. I had her figured out in an hour. I've been watching you for days now, and I still can't figure you out."

She felt a completely irrational swell of pleasure at this knowledge that she was deep enough, complicated enough, to be a challenge to this charming, intelligent, urbane man.

He smiled. "You like that idea."

"I do not." She felt trapped against the wall, with Hall's body just a few breaths away from hers. "And would you please back up?"

"Why?"

"Because you're not allowed to touch anyone else while you're a Potential. It's a punishable offense."

"I touched you this afternoon," he murmured, his eyes caressing her face. "But I'm not touching you now."

"It feels like you are." She was trembling now, her body reacting to his proximity, even as she realized that he wasn't actually touching her anywhere.

She was suddenly terrified. She shouldn't be feeling this. She shouldn't be reacting this way. She had no idea who this man was or what he was up to here.

Hall raised a hand and very lightly grazed her cheekbone with his finger. She felt a delicious little tug inside her as her fear transformed into relaxed pleasure. She heard herself moaning as she arched against the hall, her tightened nipples slightly brushing against his chest.

She moaned again, liking how it felt, liking how she felt right now.

Hall's eyes went hot as he stared at her. She liked that too.

"How are you doing this?" she whispered, wondering what was wrong with her body, that it was acting this way.

"Doing what?"

"Whatever you're doing to make me feel this way."

"I'm not doing anything. It's all you."

"No, it's not. Sex isn't my thing. I told you that before."

He leaned in a little closer, his hand now planted against the wall. "Sex is everyone's thing. You just need to find the right partner."

"You need to save your energy for my sister. That's what you're here for."

"What if I don't want her anymore?"

The hoarse sound of his voice sliced through her with another wave of sensation. But she managed to think clearly enough to say, "It's too late."

Then suddenly she realized it was true. Her life—as well as his—was now dictated by the laws of Evalon. He'd declared himself for her sister. He could never be anything else to Kyla. If her sister rejected him, then he would have to leave the planet forever.

And Kyla could never leave. Never have him.

The truth of it slammed into her like a hammer. She was acting just like those foolish, spineless women she despised.

She pushed him back so she could move away from the wall and ran down the hall, away from him. She needed to get away. She needed to never talk to him again.

He wasn't for her, and she shouldn't even want him.

She took another shot of her medication, mostly so she could sleep. It didn't really work though. She tossed and turned in bed all night, dreaming about Hall's eyes, Hall's laugh, Hall's hands touching her body.

And when she woke up, she felt terrible, so she decided to spend the day in bed.

At least, that way, she wouldn't have to see Hall again.

~

"Seriously, Hall, you're being stupid," Lenna said, shaking her head at him with an uncharacteristically disapproving expression.

Hall had known Lenna for a long time. She was usually easygoing and didn't care about whatever he did in his personal life. It was one of the reasons they'd always gotten along well.

"I'm just having a little fun," he said, ensuring that his expression was nonchalant, although he felt rather defensive, which wasn't like him at all. "It's not going to cause any trouble."

"It will. Not only is she completely out of your league, but if anyone sees you pursuing her, you could endanger your position in the palace. And then we might as well give up and go home because our job will never get done."

"I'm not going to lose my position. I have ways of getting people to change their minds, remember?"

Lenna rolled her eyes. "Yes, I remember. But that's a different kind of danger, and you wouldn't have to rely on it if you'd just be smart. I've never seen you like this before. What is it about this girl that's got you going like this?"

She still looked faintly annoyed but also curious now. She had absolutely no interest in Hall herself. They'd had sex a few times when they'd first met, but then they'd discovered they were in the same business and decided to partner up. After that, any personal interest they'd had in each other had disappeared in the face of what was much more important to both of them. Business.

"I don't know," Hall admitted, rubbing his jaw and feeling uncharacteristically foolish. "I really don't know. Haven't you ever been slammed in the face by something you just had to have?"

Lenna arched her eyebrows. "Maybe one of those new galaxy-class cruisers. Or that ruby we almost got our hands on in Karna. Definitely not a man."

Hall huffed in faint amusement. "Well, it's never happened to me before either."

"I thought you said you were just having fun."

"I am," he said quickly. "I know nothing is going to come of it. I've got to do something for the next few weeks until we can get out of here. What does it matter?"

"It matters because it could put you in danger. Or, even worse, it could put *me* in danger. And it matters because I don't believe you when you say it's just for fun. I've watched you chase women on every planet from here to Earth, and you've never been like this before."

Hall wondered if that was true. It made him nervous— and just a little bit excited. "It'll be fine, Lenna. Let me handle my own business."

She shook her head again as she stood up. "Okay. If you say so. We better not meet again like this until next week. You should probably stay inside the palace walls as much as possible since you're not being too smart about other matters."

"Fine. We should be all set anyway. I'll toss a note over the wall if anything else comes up."

He wanted to get back inside the walls anyway. He wanted to see if Kyla was walking today. If not, maybe he could at least see her across the room at Court this evening.

He waved to Lenna and felt a churning in his stomach.

She might be right. He might be stupid.

It might be best if he avoid Kyla as much as possible. But even as he had the thought, he knew he couldn't follow through with it.

THREE

Kyla spent the next four days keeping to herself. She didn't go down to Court in the evenings, and she didn't participate in the royal picnic or the flutterball matches that were scheduled at the palace that week.

Perhaps it was irrational to be so flustered by a man she barely knew, but she didn't want to encounter him again and end up feeling even worse.

She was used to reading and lounging and staring out at the world beyond the palace gates—often for weeks at a time, with no interruptions—but she was getting bored and restless this week. She'd learned how to make shoes as a child from her father, and a few years ago, she'd started making boots again in her spare time, starting with leather and sewing and cobbling them with her dad's old tools. Although it was the pastime she enjoyed most, she couldn't even focus on the work.

She kept thinking about Hall, and that meant she couldn't relax.

She wondered who he really was. She wondered what he was really doing here. He didn't seem like the normal kind of man who declared himself a Potential. They were usually shallow and lazy, looking for a rich woman to support them in style. Men had no political power in Evalon, so the more ambitious and intelligent men rarely wanted the role of consort.

Midweek, she was sitting on her private terrace, with a book and a citrus drink, trying to enjoy the lovely afternoon. She couldn't concentrate on her story though, and eventually she put the book down and looked down at the courtyard—

wondering what Hall was doing, wondering when her sister would choose him for her weekly partner.

The thought made her feel vaguely sick, but she really needed to get used to it.

She sighed deeply and sipped her drink, trying to relax. But she put her glass down quickly when she saw a familiar figure appear in the courtyard, apparently having come out of the back door of the palace that she always used. She was too far away to see his face clearly, but she recognized his lean body, his dark hair, the way he carried himself.

It was Hall. He was leaving through the back door, like he had something to hide.

Kyla jumped to her feet, dropping her book and running into her dressing room to change quickly from her thin day dress to the trousers and boots she wore for walking.

She knew where he was probably going. She didn't have to keep up with him. She'd follow him without risk of being caught and maybe get a better sense of what he was up to.

She was even prepared to climb the wall and go into the village if she had to although she hadn't dared to breach the perimeter since she was fourteen.

Three minutes later she was hurrying down the back stairs and slipping out the door, telling the guard posted there she was just taking a walk.

The guard's name was Iram. He knew her and knew her habits. He just grinned as he gave her a little bow. "Glad to see you feeling better, miss."

Kyla had been using illness as an excuse to hibernate this week, as she often did. There was no other way she could get out of the many tedious social events expected of her.

"Thank you," she called with a wave, walking quickly toward the trail in the woods that led to the corner of the wall that offered the only escape route.

She walked quickly, so she was slightly out of breath when she reached sight of the vine-covered section of wall. She paused in the cover of the trees. Hall must already be up and over since he wasn't in sight.

She waited as a security drone buzzed by. She was going to climb the wall. She would be in serious trouble if she got caught, but if she could find out what Hall was doing, it would be worth it.

She waited a minute or two until two more drones flew by, and she ran for the wall, climbing up quickly by clinging to the vines. It wasn't easy work, but with a little effort, she pulled herself up toward the top.

She stopped abruptly when she heard voices, coming from the other side of the wall.

"It's about time you showed up." The voice was Hall's. She would recognize it anywhere.

"Sorry. I had to make sure no one was around. If communicators were allowed on this backwoods planet, it would be a lot easier for us to get the job done." The second voice was female. Kyla had no way of knowing for sure, but she would bet it was the blond woman he'd met in the café last week.

"Well, they're not, and there was no way for me to smuggle one past the palace scanners. So let's be quick. It's dangerous for us to meet like this, especially so close to the palace grounds."

Kyla held her body perfectly still, clinging to the vines on the wall. She had about two and a half minutes before another security drone came by, but she had to hear more of this conversation.

"I know. I know," the woman said. "I ran into a few problems though. We're going to have to use another guy."

"Damn it. I thought you had it worked out."

"I thought so too. Anyway, I'll need a little more time."

"Shit." Hall's mutter was soft but intense.

"Hey, you have the easy job, remember?"

"Easy? I'm basically part of a harem."

The woman chuckled. "That was your idea."

"There was no other way to get into the palace unsuspected."

Kyla's heart dropped at this proof that he was here under false pretenses. She'd suspected it, but that was different from knowing it for sure.

"I find it quite amusing that her Lady Highness still hasn't chosen you. Maybe you're not as irresistible as you think."

"I've been hiding my natural charm on purpose." Hall sounded amused now too.

"If you say so. Anyway, I'll find someone else as soon as I can. Definitely before our last two weeks are up. I don't like this planet."

"It's not that bad."

"Don't think I don't know why you want to stay longer."

"What are you talking about?"

"You know exactly what I'm talking about, and you said it was just for fun."

Kyla blinked in surprise, wishing they'd speak with a few more details. Nothing wrong with a little more exposition in a conversation she was eavesdropping on.

"I meant what I said." Hall's tone was unnaturally stiff.

"Maybe you think you do. But I'm telling you to get it under control. We've got a job to do."

"I know. I'm doing the job. Nothing is going to distract me."

"See that it doesn't. You can have all the fun you want, with whomever you want, between jobs. But if it starts to get in the way of work, I'll have to find another partner."

Kyla suddenly realized that the drone would be coming by any second. She climbed down the vines as quietly as she could, barely making it back to the grass by the time the drone came by. She crouched down, pretending to be adjusting her boot so the guards watching wouldn't think she was doing anything wrong.

She couldn't hear the conversation on the other side of the wall as well from this position, but she thought she heard Hall say, "No you won't. You'll never find another partner as callous and mercenary as me."

Kyla felt heavy and shaky as she straightened up and moved away from the wall. She still had no idea what Hall was trying to do here, but at least she had confirmation that he was here with ulterior motives.

It may not be bad. He could be doing something against the law but not actually a threat to Evalon or its people. There were a lot of trivial laws here that meant almost nothing. Kyla didn't want to think that he was here actively working against her or her world.

She hated the thought. It made her sick.

She hadn't yet decided what to do when she heard a rustling on the other side of the wall. Then Hall appeared on top, glancing both ways before he dropped down to the grass, not far from where she was standing.

He was obviously surprised to see her. His eyes widened as he straightened up. For just a moment he looked unnerved before relaxed good humor filled his face. "I didn't expect to see you," he drawled, walking toward her as his smile got warmer.

She frowned and narrowed her eyes. "I can see that."

"Why do you look so disapproving? You already know I've been over the wall before. I don't like to be penned in."

"Maybe. But I want to know *why* you've been over the wall. If you don't tell me, then I'm going to report you to the guards."

His smile faded. "You wouldn't do that."

"Yes, I would." She stepped back when he moved even closer. His presence still did terrifying things to her body, even knowing what she knew about him. "Tell me now, or I'll report you."

His expression changed again, becoming almost wistful, as if he saw something in her that he appreciated even though it gave him trouble. "You really should be careful, Kyla. Not all men are as kindhearted as me. If someone was really up to no good and you threatened them like that, you might end up hurt."

She was breathless but not really from fear. It was a different kind of excitement. "Are you going to hurt me?"

"Of course not. I'm not that kind of man."

"I think you could hurt someone if you wanted to."

"Sure," he said with a half smile. "To defend myself. But I'm not a violent man. I'm too meek and gentle for that."

She shook her head, trying not to laugh at his insouciance. The man was shameless even when confronted with his wrongdoing.

And the most ridiculous thing was she found him more attractive now than she had before, as if part of her liked his shamelessness.

"There's nothing meek and gentle about you," she said, managing to keep her expression from softening. "Now tell me what you're up to, or I'll go report you right now."

He let out a breath. "I'm a freelancer. A mercenary. I do a variety of jobs for money."

This rang true to her. He seemed exactly like a mercenary should, if maybe a little too intelligent and cerebral. "What kind of jobs?"

"Various. In this case, Evalon has a number of very stringent import/export laws, and my client needs to get certain… goods off-world without attracting attention."

She blinked. "Smuggling?"

He nodded, his eyes holding hers.

She believed him. She couldn't help but believe him. It *felt* true, in addition to making sense logically. She was overwhelmed with relief that he wasn't actually here to hurt anyone.

She didn't care about import/export laws. She didn't care about smuggling, as long as it wasn't dangerous materials. Her first impression of Hall hadn't been wrong if all he was doing here was smuggling.

"You work alone?" she asked, testing him to see if he would tell her the truth.

"No. I have a partner who usually works with me. She's been in town handling our exit strategy while I'm working the palace."

She blew out a breath, feeling better about the whole world.

"So are you going to report me?" he asked, giving her a faint smile. "If you are, I'd appreciate your giving me a small head start to get out of here."

She shook her head. "You're not smuggling weapons or explosives, are you?"

"No. Wool from your special sheep."

Her lips parted as she understood. The wool was known and desired in all the surrounding galaxies, and there was a 90 percent tax on it, as the Coalition gouged the buyers of the best products in their control.

"I see," she said, unable to keep from smiling back at him. "I get it. As long as no one gets hurt, you can do your thing."

"I knew I liked you." His smile warmed so much it made her breathless.

"Well, the verdict is still out on whether or not I like you."

"You do."

She tried to frown but couldn't quite manage it. Her heart was racing with excitement again. "I certainly don't like that kind of arrogance."

He reached up to brush her cheekbone with his fingers, the way he had the other evening. She waited to feel that inner tug but didn't feel it this time. All she felt was pleasure and more excitement. "Yes, you do," he murmured.

Her knees felt weak, and she swayed toward him, and there was no telling what would have happened had he not glanced up at the position of the sun. "Damn. I better get back. There are all those ridiculous bathing rituals I have to go through before Court."

"You're the one who thought it a good idea to declare himself a Potential."

"It was the only way I could get into the palace for any length of time."

"One week, you might actually get chosen by my sister, you know."

"I've lucked out so far. I only need two more weeks."

That fit exactly with what she'd overheard him say over the wall—another confirmation that he was telling the truth. "You're not really her type, so you have that going for you."

"Good. Any advice on how to continue to avoid her notice?"

"She doesn't like smart men."

"Ah." He grinned. "That works in my favor then."

Kyla couldn't help but chuckle. "More arrogance. I guess there's not an end to it from you."

"No. Not really. But I'm fortunate that you like smart, arrogant men."

She gasped. "I do not."

He brushed her hair back from her face. "Yes, you do." His smile faded into something deep and almost sober. "I don't think you've ever let yourself think about what you like, what you want. Maybe it's time that you do."

She lost her breath again, for a different reason this time. The words filled her mind, followed by all kinds of questions. He was right. She'd never thought much about it since she'd never had the freedom to pursue what she really wanted.

She didn't have the freedom now either. But she wanted it. She really wanted it. More than ever.

When she felt herself leaning toward him again, lost in his gaze, she remembered herself in time to straighten up and say, "You should be getting back. They'll kick you off the planet if you're not where you're supposed to be in time."

"Yeah."

They started down the trail together, and even in the silence, it felt like she knew him for real, knew him in a way she'd not really known anyone.

He would be leaving in two weeks. And she would be left here, with nothing really different about her life.

"What just made you sad?" he asked.

"Nothing."

"I was watching you. You thought of something that made you sad."

"It's not really your business."

"I told you before. You feel like my business."

"Then your feelings are leading you astray."

The corner of his mouth tilted up. "I guess they do that from time to time."

"Yes. They do."

They walked in silence until they reached the edge of the woods. Then she glanced up at him. "You go in first since you have to get back to your quarters."

"Okay. Maybe I'll see you tonight then."

"If you do, it will be across the room since you can't leave your section."

"I know. It's very inconvenient. But I'd like to see you anyway. It's time for you to stop hiding."

She gasped and stiffened her shoulders. "I haven't been hiding."

He leaned over and brushed a very light kiss against her cheekbone, exactly where he'd stroked her before. "Yes, you have," he whispered. "And it's time for you to come out of your room."

He started to pull away, but then he glanced his lips against her skin again as if he couldn't keep himself from doing it again.

It felt delicious. She was trembling all over. And then she felt that little inner tug again, and the last of her reservations transformed into a flood of deep pleasure. She moaned shamelessly and reached out to cling to his shoulders since her legs wouldn't support her otherwise.

Hall made a throaty sound in his throat as if it felt just as good to him. Then he jerked away and muttered, "I'll see you tonight."

He was gone before she could say a word in response.

She waited a few minutes before she went back into the palace. Iram greeted her in his normal friendly manner, obviously suspecting nothing of the fact that she was coming back just after Hall.

No one would expect for them to have met up. No one would expect them to talk. No one ever expected any man to pay attention to her—just as she never went after any man.

She'd always been that way, but maybe she wanted it to be different. Maybe Hall was right about her.

It wasn't as easy as it sounded, however, since her days, her whole life, was dictated by her position in the royal family and the rigid rituals of her world.

She was connected to Evalon even though life here didn't really suit her. It wasn't like she could just pick up and leave.

Could she?

Not for Hall though. She hardly knew him. Even if he offered, she couldn't trust her whole future to him.

She might be falling for him, despite her best efforts, but she wasn't that foolish.

She returned to her room and decided to take a bath. As her server drew hot water and scented it with lavender oil, Kyla stared at herself in the mirror.

She looked different. Her cheeks were flushed, and there was a glint in her eyes that she liked. Even her hair seemed brighter than it used to.

She was almost, almost pretty.

Maybe Hall would think so when he saw her tonight.

~

The next afternoon, Hall decided to go out for a walk, right about the time Kyla had the day before.

He'd decided the only way to cure his fascination with Kyla was to actually get her into bed. And that would only happen if he could get her alone since she was so turned off by Court and all the blatant sexuality that characterized it.

He knew she was attracted to him. He'd felt it deeply, vividly, after he'd opened a connection with her when she'd run out of Court on the last Feast Day. If he could get her to trust him, then she'd open up enough to give in to her attraction to him.

Once he had sex with her, she'd be like any other woman to him, and he'd be able to leave this planet without looking back once their job was done.

But the first step was to get some more time to talk to her in private, and the only place that was possible in such a well-guarded palace was in the woods.

So he went out after lunch and waited near the trail she used. To his relief, she came out even sooner than he'd expected.

She looked young and fresh and pretty in a simple green tunic with her long hair pulled back into one long braid. His heart did a silly little leap in his chest when he saw her.

He moved onto the trail, facing the opposite direction as her so it would look like he was on his way back from a walk.

She jerked to a stop when the trail curved enough for her to see him. "What are you doing here?"

"I was taking a walk. What does it look like?"

She frowned. "Were you out to meet your partner again?"

"No. We don't meet every day. That would be foolish."

"Yes. It would. So you're really just taking a walk?"

"Why do you sound so surprised?"

"I don't know. It seems like such an innocent pastime."

"And I'm not innocent?"

She almost, almost smiled. "No. You're definitely not."

"Well, you'll have to be innocent enough for both of us."

"I'm not innocent," she said, her eyes wide.

"I thought you said you hadn't had sex."

"I haven't, but what does that have to do with anything? Since I was twelve years old, I've watched men fuck women, men fuck men, women fuck women, and groups of three and four fuck each other. There's not much I haven't seen and I don't know. I'm definitely not innocent."

He thought about that—what such a background would do to a child. No wonder she was so turned off sex. It was a wonder her sister still loved it so much. "Okay. I'll agree to that. But you're something... you're... untouched." He had no idea why he was talking like this to her. It was revealing too much about his thoughts regarding her, and it wasn't really getting them where he wanted them to be.

She gave a little shrug. "If you say so. I don't really feel untouched though. I feel…"

When she drifted off, he asked, "You feel what?"

"I don't know. Tired, bored of it all. There's got to be something more than just this. There's *got* to be."

This would have been the perfect opportunity for him to start building up the idea of him introducing the world of sex to her in a way she'd never experienced, but he couldn't bring himself to do it. She was being perfectly genuine with him, and he wanted to match it somehow. "I don't know," he admitted. "I've traveled all over. I've seen hellholes and paradises and everything in between. And I haven't found much more than this. Take what you're given, and enjoy the time you have. It's the only philosophy that works."

She shook her head. "I don't know. It doesn't feel right to me. It feels like something has been taken away."

He smiled, feeling connected to her even more deeply than he had before. "Well, if you tell me what it is, I can help you go find it."

She smiled back.

"Can I walk with you?"

"I thought you already walked."

"Sure," he said easily. "But I can walk some more. I don't have anything to do until I have to endure more hours of preparation for Court."

She chuckled. "You're the one who signed up for it."

"I know. I'm not really complaining. But I could use another walk—and some better company."

"Okay. Fine."

She trusted him. Maybe not completely but definitely more than she had before.

He should use it to his advantage somehow, but he couldn't really make his mind work that way.

The truth was he mostly felt... proud.

~

The next day, Kyla spent all morning looking forward to her walk. There was no reason to expect Hall to join her again today, but she thought it was possible.

She really hoped he would.

She made a point not to hurry, however, as she walked downstairs and out the back door of the palace as usual, giving Iram a friendly wave as she stepped outside.

It took a lot of effort to maintain the pose of nonchalance as she walked toward the head of the trail through the woods, and she gave a little jump—more of pleasure than surprise—when she turned the first curve in the trail and saw Hall.

He stood leaning against a tree, and he was obviously waiting for her since he straightened up as she came into sight.

"You're here again?" she said, pleased when her voice sounded cool and casual.

"Naturally. Talking to you is the most interesting part of my days."

"Well, I'm so glad I can provide you a little entertainment." She kept walking down the trail as he fell in step with her.

"I'd say enjoyment is a more appropriate word than entertainment."

She glanced up to check his face, which was smiling and looked genuine. She was ridiculously pleased by the words, by the idea that he enjoyed spending time with her.

"Do you just walk up and back on this trail every day?" Hall asked, bending over to pick up a fallen branch.

"No. I usually start off in this direction, but sometimes I walk through the orchards and lavender fields. Sometimes I just climb a tree and look out at the village."

"Seriously? Why do you do that?"

"It's interesting to watch people. I almost never leave the palace grounds, you know."

His expression changed. "I know. That's got to get old really quick. What do you do with the rest of your time?"

"I read a lot. Or make boots."

"Boots? Seriously?" He looked interested and surprised.

"Yeah. I made these." She stuck out her foot to show him.

"Wow," he breathed. "They're great. You're really good at that."

"It's just for fun," she said, flushing with pleasure. "But it's nice to actually make things with my hands."

"I guess so." He paused and then asked in a different tone, "What tree do you climb when you watch people?"

"I'll show you."

She had no qualms about showing him her favorite tree. He would eventually be gone, and it wasn't like he was going to try to take her favorite position to people watch.

If he wanted to people watch, once he left Evalon, all he had to do was step outside.

"It's this tree," she said a few minutes later when she reached the big tree with a few thick, low branches.

"It's huge."

"Yeah, but it's easy to climb." To show him, she pulled herself up on the lowest branch, grabbing the one above it until she could stand on the branch.

Hall grinned at her, looking faintly surprised and delighted, like he'd been given an unexpected gift. He grabbed the low branch too and pulled himself up until he was standing on the branch beside her. Together they climbed up the rest of the way until they reached the flattened branch that made such a good seat.

"See," she said, gesturing out over the wall in the distance. "You can see half the village from here."

"What you need are binoculars."

"I have some," she said, grinning at him and showing him the binoculars she kept hidden in the hole in the tree. She didn't mention that she'd seen him in the café with the blonde that day. It would give away her advantage.

"How long have you been climbing this tree?" he asked.

"For years. Since I was a little girl."

"And you were never tempted to just hop on over the wall?" He was leaning back against the thick trunk beside her, and they were sitting very close together in order for them both to fit on the branch.

"Of course I was. It was against the rules, and that made it even more tempting. I actually did a few times, but the punishments got worse and worse, and eventually it didn't seem worth it. There was no real adventure to be had in the village anyway. So I'd just sit in this tree and look over the wall and dream about how it would feel to be free."

She gave a little start as she finished the sentence, surprised and unnerved that she'd spoken so openly to a man she didn't know and didn't trust.

He didn't appear to think it was strange though. With a thoughtful expression, he murmured, "You didn't feel free even with all the luxuries you could ask for?"

"You can have all kinds of luxuries, but if you're trapped in a palace, you're still trapped in a palace."

"They wouldn't let you out even if you asked?"

"Yes, they'd let me out, but I'd only be able to go certain places and do certain things. It doesn't feel free when your life is scripted that way. I can't go where I want. I can't be who I want to be."

"Who would you want to be?" It sounded like he really wanted to know.

She gave a slightly bitter shrug. "I don't even know." Then she shook her head hard. "Sorry. I don't mean to sound like all I do is complain. I know I have a good life, compared to the majority of people. But I guess everyone wants what they don't have."

"Yeah. I think that's right. And I sure wouldn't want to be stuck here all my life. A fancy prison is still a prison."

She gave him a little smile, ridiculously pleased that he'd understood. "I guess you've never felt like that."

"Like what? Like I was in a prison." He gave a strange little laugh. "I've definitely felt that way."

"But you can go anywhere you like, do anything you want, can't you? You've traveled all over, haven't you?"

"What makes you think that?"

"You said so yesterday. And you're a freelancer, aren't you? You look like you've lived... hard."

His laughter this time was more genuine. "Thanks. But sure, I've traveled and experienced all kinds of things, but there are other ways of feeling bound by your own life."

"How do you feel bound?" She didn't really expect him to answer.

"When anyone meets me, they always assume I'm only one thing." He quirked his eyebrows at her.

"Let me guess. They think you're a handsome, charming playboy, don't they?"

He gave a self-deprecating flip of his hand that was clearly an admission.

"So does that change when they get to know you?"

"Sometimes." For the first time, his expression sobered. "But when someone really gets to know me, then they're always afraid of me."

This wasn't at all what she'd expected. "What? What do you mean? Why are they afraid of you?"

He met her eyes and gave a half shrug. "Certain skills can be... dangerous."

She didn't doubt for a minute that this man could be dangerous, and he was probably an expert at weapons and fighting. But she felt like she was getting to know him better, and she wasn't afraid of him. She didn't really understand what he was talking about.

"Yeah," she said slowly, "but they're only dangerous if they're used against people, right? Why do they always assume you're going to use your skills against them? I wouldn't assume that."

"Wouldn't you?" he asked softly.

"No. I'm not afraid of you."

With a little smile, he reached up and stroked her cheekbone with his knuckles. "Thank you for that, but I don't think you really know me yet."

She had no argument to that one, so she was silent for a minute, thinking about what he'd just said.

Finally she sighed and said, "Honestly, sometimes I wish someone was actually afraid of me. At least it would prove I have some depth."

"Of course you have depth," he said, sounding surprised.

"Sometimes I feel like these woods—artificially created for a very limited purpose and only allowed to grow within preconceived limits. And mostly just for show. And even that I'm not any good at."

"Now, you know that's not true."

"Yes, it really is."

"Because you don't look like your sister? There are different kinds of beauty, you know. And yours is like a violet next to a peony. One might get most of the attention, but that's not because the other is less beautiful. It's just worth a harder pursuit."

Kyla peered at him and saw nothing but sincerity in his eyes. She couldn't help but smile. She'd never received a better compliment in her life, and it didn't seem just like empty praise.

Starting to feel self-conscious, she decided it was safest if she change the subject. "Where were you born?"

Hall didn't seem to mind the shift. He relaxed against the trunk and said, "On a little planet no one has ever heard of. It was naturally habitable though, so no artificial habitation generators. My parents owned a vineyard."

"Really? Did they make wine?"

"Yes. Really fine wine. They had a small but very exclusive market. They were never rich, but they loved the grapes and they loved the wine."

"So I guess you know all about wine then."

"Oh yes." He smiled, as if the thought of it made him happy.

"How's the wine in our Court?"

"Not bad, as far as replicated stuff goes. It's just a shallow reflection of the real thing though."

"Yeah. I guess so. I've never had the real thing."

"You need to remedy that before you die."

She doubted that would ever happen, but she did like the idea. "So is the vineyard still around?"

"No. My uncle sold it off when my parents died."

"Oh no! How old were you?"

"Eleven. I was sent to live with my grandmother after that."

"Where did she live?"

"She lived on Earth. In the ugliest part of the concrete jungle that planet has turned into."

"That doesn't sound good after the vineyard."

"In some ways it was alright. My grandmother... She had similar... gifts to me. But she didn't have very much else to offer me. I had to learn to make it on my own."

All the history he was sharing was fitting together in her mind, turning him into a whole person, a person she understood. "I guess you became self-sufficient early then."

"Yes." He was smiling faintly, but there was a familiar glint of bitterness in his eyes that she'd seen there before. "I told myself if I could ever get out of that life, I would start moving and never stop. That world felt like a prison to me, and I was desperate to be free."

She nodded. "Kind of like me, only my prison was a little more comfortable."

"Exactly," Hall agreed.

"I guess maybe that feeling isn't all that unusual," she said, thinking as the words came out. "For the life we're given to feel like... like shackles."

He met her eyes and held her gaze for a really long time. Finally he breathed, "Yeah."

"At least you managed to get out."

"Did I?"

"Well, you're not stuck in that ugly part of Earth anymore, are you?"

"True. But I don't really feel very different. I just can't shake that feeling of being... bound. Last year, I was in a... a really bad situation. I came pretty close to killing myself. I got out of it, but everything seems tainted after that. Like nothing I used to enjoy is the same." He sighed and closed his eyes. "It feels like I'm still in prison."

She gazed at him, understanding his bitterness, fatigue, disillusionment better than she would have expected.

After a moment, he gave a wry chuckle as if he'd just remembered who he was and what he was doing. "Anyway, none of that is really relevant at the moment."

She didn't like that he'd brushed aside their conversation that way. "I think it is. I think it's relevant. It's funny that we both kind of feel the same. Maybe we're just doing life wrong."

This idea seemed to strike a chord in Hall. His brows drew together, like he was mulling over what she'd just said.

No one in all her life had listened to her the way Hall had. No one had taken her words so seriously, like she might actually be saying something wise, something worthwhile.

She suddenly felt too close to him, too exposed, like she was stripped naked in front of him—far deeper than anything physical.

It was terrifying. She'd never experienced it before. She straightened up with a little gasp and started to climb back down the tree.

"I didn't realize it was so late," she said, trying to sound natural. "I better be getting back."

Hall looked like he'd been woken up abruptly, like he couldn't quite focus yet. "Yeah. Me too."

When they'd both reached the ground, he reached out to put his hand on her back, an automatic gesture to guide her back to the trail. She jerked away from his touch without thinking, still scared of the intimacy she'd felt earlier.

"Sorry," she said with a nervous laugh. "You just scared me."

His eyes never left her face. "I know I did."

She didn't know what exactly he meant by that, but it had sounded significant.

She decided the best thing to do would be to get back to the safety of her room.

FOUR

Eight days later, Kyla was sitting out on her terrace, breathing in a fresh breeze and waiting rather impatiently for when she could go on her walk.

She'd been walking every afternoon, and each day Hall had shown up to meet her. They'd laughed and walked and talked about all kinds of things—from Coalition politics to her childhood—and each morning she woke up looking forward to seeing him again.

She knew it was wrong. She knew she'd been lucky so far that Patrice hadn't chosen Hall for her weekly partner. She knew their friendship or acquaintance or whatever this was couldn't last. But she couldn't seem to stay inside when the afternoons came around. She'd been scared at first, but her interest had overcome her fear. This was the first time in ages she'd actually been excited about anything.

She was going to hold on to it as long as she could.

There was still another hour before she could expect him to be out, so she closed her eyes and tried to relax, tried not to feel jittery, tried not to wonder what they would talk about today.

Or whether he would touch her.

He hadn't. Not since she'd jerked away from him when he'd tried to put his hand on her back. She didn't know why he hadn't. Maybe he thought she really didn't want his touch.

There was a lot she didn't know about him.

No matter how much she told herself he was a smuggler—and may be hiding other secrets and so she really couldn't trust him—it still felt like he was telling her the truth.

She was usually good at reading people. She wouldn't be so mistaken about Hall.

She was mulling over the endless questions when a voice from behind her surprised her. "I hope you don't have a headache."

Kyla turned and smiled at her sister, despite the slightly impatient tone of her voice. "No. I don't. Just enjoying the breeze."

"It's a little chilly," Patrice replied with a frown, pulling her velvet shawl up around her shoulders as she came out and sat down beside Kyla. "I wish they'd keep it summer longer."

"They have to work different seasons into the climate or most of our plants would never grow right. Besides, I love it when it finally gets cooler."

"You would. You've always been contrary in all things." Patrice was smiling slightly as she said the words, so they didn't come off as a complete insult.

"No argument here."

"You're coming to the masquerade tonight, aren't you?"

Kyla rolled her eyes. "I'm not sure. You know I hate big parties like that."

"I know. But you need to be there. I've planned a special surprise."

"What surprise?" Kyla's voice cracked slightly, as she was hit with a shiver of worry. Patrice looked too pleased with herself. That was never a good sign.

"You have to wait and see."

"Please don't do anything foolish."

"What would be foolish?"

"You know exactly what I mean. Following any of the old royal traditions, making too big a deal about being Empress. There could be Coalition eyes watching, you know—especially if everyone is wearing masks."

Patrice waved a dismissive hand. "They're not going to care about a party."

"Yes, they will—if they think you're flouting their authority. Patrice, I'm serious. Even Tor mentioned that—"

"Yes, I've seen you choosing Commander Tor for your partner several times now," Patrice interrupted, her expression clearing into a characteristic teasing smile. "Is there something I should know?"

"No. Tor is my friend, and I can sit with him at Court without him expecting anything to happen. But he knows the Coalition, and even he said you should be careful."

"I'm always careful."

"No, you're not. You never take advice. You're just like Mother and Grandmother. But just because we could get away with certain things fifty years ago doesn't mean we can get away with them now. Please, Patrice, don't do anything dangerous. Promise me."

Patrice laughed and leaned over to kiss Kyla's cheek. "I promise, silly. Don't worry. And you should come tonight. It's going to be fun. I'm even going to let the Potentials mingle in disguise."

Kyla couldn't help but straighten her spine at this piece of news. "Really? That's not like you."

"I know." Patrice's lovely pink mouth pursed mischievously, showing her dimple. "I've never been inclined to share. But I thought it would be fun tonight to let them mingle with the masses and give other women a taste of what they can never have."

Kyla felt kind of sick at those words. She knew her sister was ostensibly teasing, but there was a reality underlying the words that couldn't be denied. Her sister had always been slightly selfish, slightly possessive, very territorial. She'd been raised that way. It wasn't even her fault.

But Hall belonged to Patrice. He'd declared himself so, whether or not he meant it, whether or not he had an underlying purpose.

Any time Kyla spent with Hall was a taste of what she could never have.

She sighed and told herself to be reasonable—that she'd known this truth all along.

"You must come tonight," Patrice added. "I thought you'd been in a good mood for a couple of weeks, but now you're looking a little depressed. A party will do you good."

"I'll think about it." Kyla was having even more doubts now about attending, knowing Hall would be in the ballroom with a mask on.

"No, you're not going to think about it. You're going to promise me right now that you'll come. I'm your sister, and I need your support."

Kyla shook her head. "You don't need anyone's support."

"Of course I do. Everything is more fun if you're around." Patrice's eyes were wide and genuine, and Kyla was sure she meant them. They might not be close, but they were family, and that meant something to both of them.

Kyla smiled and said, "Okay. I'll come tonight."

"You promise."

"I promise."

Patrice clapped her hands. "Wonderful! I'll send you my dresser to figure out something for you to wear. You can work with her all afternoon."

"I don't want to work with her—"

"Of course you must. You can't go to the masquerade in one of your normal outfits. Everyone will know who you are."

"But not all afternoon—"

"It will take as long as it takes."

Kyla sighed, resigning herself to the fact that she may have to miss her walk with Hall this afternoon. Maybe she could finish with the dresser quickly—although that had never happened in all the time she'd known the fussy woman.

Patrice was grinning. "I'll send her down in an hour or so, as soon as she finishes with me. We've mostly already decided what I'm going to wear anyway. Oh, it's going to be a fabulous night. No one will ever forget it."

Those words didn't excite Kyla. They worried her.

After all, unforgettable nights weren't always good.

~

Several hours later, Kyla was walking into the ballroom, wearing an emerald-green silk gown and a feathered mask.

The music and dancing had already begun—as had any number of erotic activities taking place on the sidelines of the room.

She stood still, gazing around and trying to recognize people she knew—one in particular—but it was harder than expected. Everyone wore mostly full masks that covered their faces down to their mouths—some even went lower—and it wasn't always easy to recognize someone's body in the swirl of lush fabrics and heady motion.

It was dizzying—wild in a way she'd never really liked.

She'd been stupid to promise her sister she'd attend. She didn't want to be here. She'd already missed her walk with Hall today, and now she had to be here, in a flurry of scent and color and sound. She hoped she wasn't getting a migraine.

She moved along the wall, looking for somewhere fairly quiet to stand where she wouldn't be confronted with gyrating bodies. It was a hopeless cause though, so she finally just stopped with her back to the wall when she could find a little clear space.

Beside her a woman was leaning against the wall with a man kneeling in front of her, his head beneath her skirt. She was flushed and moaning, and she smiled at Kyla beneath her mask. "Would you like to join us?"

Kyla smiled back and murmured her decline, feeling a familiar sick feeling at being surrounded by so much sex. She didn't want to do it with one person—she definitely didn't want to do it with two.

She sighed and pressed her back against the wall, closing her eyes and trying to will her mind away from this room. She wondered how long she had to stay to keep her promise to Patrice.

Her sister evidently had a surprise for tonight. Hopefully, it wouldn't be something too stupid.

"I was wondering if you would come," a low voice murmured, just at her ear.

Her eyes flew open, and she gasped in surprise. She knew Hall's voice, although the sight of the gray velvet mask with pointed ears that made it look like a wolf was very unnerving so close to her face.

"Where were you this afternoon?" he asked, turning her body so she was facing him.

"This is a masquerade. I don't know who you are. You must have the wrong person," she said, feeling the strangest desire to play for a minute—maybe because he sounded so entitled, so possessive.

"You know exactly who I am, and I don't have the wrong person." He reached up and stroked her hair, which she'd pulled back into a sleek bun. "You think I don't recognize your hair—or your body." His eyes lowered behind the mask and took in her clingy gown with its low neckline. "You are unmistakable."

She tried not to shiver as her body reacted to his presence, his warm gaze. "You shouldn't be talking to me."

"I'm allowed tonight. We're allowed to mingle."

"Until she calls you back."

"She hasn't done so yet." His voice changed as he added, "I missed you this afternoon. I kept waiting, but you never showed up."

She let out a breath, feeling a swell of pleasure that he sounded like he meant it. "My sister sent her dresser down to work with me on my outfit. It took hours."

"Why didn't you say no?"

"It's not worth the fuss. It's easier to just go along with things."

"Maybe. But then you don't get what you want."

He sounded different with her tonight than he had for the past week on their walks. Lately, he'd talked to her pleasantly, almost gently—but right now he sounded more forceful, even though the volume of his words never raised.

It was unnerving—as unnerving as everything else about him.

"Maybe I wanted a sexy dress for tonight."

"It is a sexy dress," he murmured, "but I know you'd rather have walked with me."

"Don't be smug. My days don't revolve around you, you know."

"Don't they? I'm disappointed."

She smiled at the teasing note in his voice but then swallowed hard as reality hit her suddenly. "Hall, we shouldn't do this. It's futile."

"What is?" He moved again so his body was trapping hers against the wall.

She wished she could see his whole face. She wanted to know what he was feeling right now. "You know what I'm talking about. You're only here for a little while, and you're a Potential. No matter what happens, you'll be leaving soon."

"And what's your point?"

"So there's no use in us being... being..."

He tilted his head down toward hers. "Being what?"

She gulped again. "Being friends, or whatever."

"I think *whatever* is a better descriptor of us. We're not just friends."

She couldn't even catch her breath now, much less try to form any words. She stared at him, meeting his eyes through their masks, and she shuddered as his face drew near to hers.

He reached up to angle her head so that he could brush her lips with his.

A surge of pleasure overwhelmed her at the first touch, and she gasped against his mouth.

Evidently encouraged by her response, he curved one of his hands around the back of her head and kissed her more deeply.

She slipped out her tongue to meet his and arched against him, supported mostly by the wall. He made a throaty sound and opened his mouth even more, causing her to do the same.

She'd never felt like this before—not once in her life. Her whole body throbbed with pleasure, with need, and with something even more powerful. She clutched at his jacket, seeing swirls of wild color behind her closed eyelids.

"Fuck, Kyla," Hall muttered, finally breaking the kiss but only to kiss an intoxicating line along her jaw and then down her throat. "I've wanted to do this from the first evening I saw you."

She moaned as he tongued her pulse point. "Then why didn't you?"

"You said you didn't like sex."

"I… I don't… I mean, I didn't…" She couldn't make her mind work. She could barely keep standing up. Her skin all over was flushed with heat.

"You wouldn't want to do this with a stranger," he mumbled, still kissing her neck as his hands started to move over her body. "You had to get to know me first."

"Oh." She gasped when he fondled her breast through the silk of her gown, teasing the nipple deliciously. "True."

"So now that you do, I can finally touch you the way I've been dying to." His body was tight, tense, hard. He pressed himself against her.

He was aroused. She could feel it against her belly. She rubbed herself against him.

He grunted as one of his hands slid up to the nape of her neck. He rubbed her there, the way he had the first day they'd met, when she'd had a migraine.

In addition to all the physical sensations, she suddenly felt something else. That inner tug she'd felt from him a few times before when he touched her.

This time it flooded her body with even more pleasure, and she cried out helplessly, completely overwhelmed with the feelings. It was like there was suddenly a channel opened from her being to his, and she was drowning in him—his pleasure as well as hers, his emotions as well as hers.

And all the building tension suddenly released inside her—in a wave that nearly knocked her off her feet. She shook against him, a throbbing beginning in her pussy and radiating out through her entire body.

"Oh, fuck!" he burst out, suddenly freezing with his mouth against her neck, his body pressed against hers. "Fuck, Kyla, I've never... never..." He was gasping and shuddering slightly. She'd never seen him so out of control.

"You've never what?" she asked hoarsely, when her mind was clear enough to think again. Her knees were buckling, so she held herself up by clinging to his shoulders.

He was still panting desperately, and his face was flushed when he finally raised it. "I've never felt anything like that."

Her blurred eyes were finally starting to clear. She blinked a few times. "Did I just... just come?"

"I think so." He cleared his throat and stroked her hot cheek with his knuckles. "It was... breathtaking."

"I didn't think it was possible without, uh, certain stimulation. What did you do?" She was thinking better now as a sated relaxation washed over her.

Something strange had happened. Something wasn't normal. She wasn't so under his spell that she couldn't recognize that much.

"I kissed you."

"I know that, but you did something else. Like you'd done it to me before." She could finally stand alone, so she pushed him away from her enough to straighten up. "Tell me what you did."

"Kyla, it's nothing." He must have gotten himself under control too, and his face had sobered under his mask. "I didn't mean to... nothing happened."

"Don't lie to me. Tell me."

Instead of the deep pleasure from moments ago—and the deeper connection she felt to him—she was suddenly cold, suspicious.

There was something about him that wasn't natural, and that meant it was dangerous.

Even to her.

He'd said that once people got to know him, they believed him to be dangerous.

This was why.

This was precisely why.

"Kyla, please." He reached out for her, but then he pulled his hand away in an awkward jerk.

Before she could say anything else, the musicians in the corner of the ballroom suddenly burst out in a fanfare. The shift in mood and sound was so startling that everyone turned to look, including Hall and Kyla.

Kyla's heart sank even more as she saw her sister walk from where she'd been dancing in the middle of the floor to the throne at the front of the room, a purple carpet spreading out before her as she walked, unrolled by two courtiers.

"Oh no," Kyla whispered, staring at her sister and recognizing the beginnings of a traditional ceremony.

A ceremony of the Empress.

It was foolish, but as long as Patrice didn't give the traditional speech, it shouldn't be the end of the world.

"What's wrong?" Hall murmured in her ear.

Kyla shook her head slightly. She wanted to confide in him, but there wasn't time, and she couldn't trust him right now anyway, now that she knew for sure he was hiding something—something other than being a smuggler.

The Court director called out for several of the most important lords and ladies to take their places, and then he called for the Potentials to come.

Patrice had warned Kyla she might do something like that—let the Potentials mingle, only to pull them away, show all the other women that they could never really have them.

That meant Hall.

"You need to go," Kyla whispered when Hall didn't move, even though all the other Potentials were making their way through the crowds to the front of the room.

He shook his head.

"You have to," she hissed. "You'll be kicked out of the palace if you don't. Go." She gave him a little shove, and he started to walk although he looked back over his shoulder at her.

Kyla made a face at him, which he may or may not have recognized beneath her mask. But he reluctantly went to take his place with the other Potentials on the far left of the throne.

Kyla held her breath as she waited for the royal court to take its traditional place around the throne.

This wasn't smart—at all. It was one of the ceremonies that had been done away with when the Coalition came into power. But hopefully it wouldn't last long and Patrice wouldn't pair it with any words.

Someone moved so he was standing beside Kyla. "She shouldn't be doing this," a familiar male voice said.

Tor. She recognized his height, the breadth of his shoulders, and his voice. "I know. I told her."

"She doesn't know who is in this room. She doesn't know where their loyalties lie."

"I *know*." Kyla's voice cracked slightly. "She won't listen."

"Her pride and silliness are going to bring down five hundred years of a royal family."

"It may be okay," Kyla said, starting to tremble in fear at the somber note in Tor's voice. "As long as she doesn't…."

She trailed off when four drumbeats sounded and Patrice started to speak.

"Four hundred and ninety-six years ago, the first Empress of Evalon took the throne."

Murmurs of reaction spilled out among the crowds, and Kyla swallowed over a rising nausea. She turned her head and hid her face briefly against Tor's shoulder. "Oh, no."

Patrice went on in words that had been said for hundreds of years at royal celebrations. "Her home world and its four surrounding planets had been destroyed by a cruel, invading force, and the brave survivors all gathered here. She built this world and declared it to be beautiful. Having survived hell, she declared this world to be paradise, with pleasure to be its only end. She declared herself Empress of the Five Destroyed Worlds. Beauty is in our nature, and pleasure is in our blood. Enjoy it now, once again—as we have for four hundred and ninety-six years. Your Empress commands it."

"Stupid," Tor was muttering under his breath. "Stupid, stupid."

Kyla hung on to his arm for support. "Is it really that bad?"

"Bad?" His eyes widened behind his plain black mask. "It's insanity. Someone will report this to a Coalition official. Someone will have to. It's outright defiance."

"Maybe everyone will be so hungover from the drunken orgies that they won't remember." Kyla looked around where the ballroom had exploded into excitement and renewed energy as the musicians began to play again.

Tor shook his head. "We can hope."

He didn't sound hopeful, and Kyla drooped against him. Her eyes flew over to the group of Potentials and landed unerringly on Hall.

He seemed to be watching her. She could tell even across the wild room. She had no idea what he might be thinking.

Clearing Hall from her mind, she focused back on what was more important. "She thinks it's just a game. She's never experienced the Coalition for real. Neither have I, for that matter."

"You don't want to. Believe me." He reached down and tilted her head up. "Their authority isn't a game to them. They've arrested people for far less and sent them to die in prison planets. It's not a pretty end."

"I know." She swallowed again and shook herself off. "I'll talk to her again tomorrow. We won't let her do it again."

"It might already be too late."

Kyla didn't answer. She had no idea what to say. She was terrified, almost dizzy from it. But Patrice had done foolish things in the past, and so far no one had ever reported it. The members of the Court were to be trusted completely, and the tourists had too good a time here to want the vacation spot to be threatened in any way.

Chances were no one would report this—despite what Tor had warned.

She suddenly felt exhausted, and she couldn't stay in the room anymore. She said goodnight to Tor and then made her way out.

Hall couldn't follow her this time. He was trapped among the rest of the Potentials, required to do the pleasure of Lady Patrice.

She couldn't believe what had happened with him earlier. She'd never felt so much pleasure in her life. But she couldn't trust it—just like she couldn't trust Hall.

And so she forced her mind away from tempting avenues of thought and instead set herself to find a way to convince Patrice not to be so stupid again.

FIVE

The next day, Kyla didn't show up on the trail where Hall normally met her.

He waited almost thirty minutes but eventually had to accept that she wasn't planning to meet with him today.

She must have been rattled by what happened between them last night. Hall was rattled too. He'd never connected with anyone so deeply before. He'd never felt so much pleasure—hers as well as his—that he'd almost come right there in the middle of a crowded room. He was confused and overwhelmed and incredibly excited, and he'd been waiting all day to see Kyla again, to feel that same way again.

But he'd tasted what she'd been feeling last night, and beneath her pleasure had been bone-deep fear. He knew that fear must be what was keeping her away from him today.

He tried to be reasonable and tell himself she might just need some time, but every fiber of his being needed to be with her again. He was tempted to storm her room and confront her, but that would be foolish in every possible way—including jeopardizing the job that had brought him here in the first place.

He remembered that she'd mentioned that she liked to walk in the afternoons but that she didn't always follow the same paths. If she wanted to avoid him today, she might just be walking somewhere else. That possibility spurred him on enough to leave the familiar trail through the woods and make a circuit around the palace, checking out some of the other locations Kyla might have ventured today.

The palace grounds were vast, however. Finding her was a long shot. He walked for an hour anyway. If he couldn't see Kyla, then the next best thing was actively looking for her.

He was wandering around the far edges of the woods, where they started to transition into cultivated meadows for the Evalonian sheep, when he saw a small building almost hidden by a cluster of evergreen trees. It was so isolated and so out of place that he immediately approached it, and his heart jumped embarrassingly when he saw there was a woman inside.

He recognized the light auburn hair, the curvy figure, the line of her jaw. Kyla. He'd found her at last. She was just standing in the building, her back to the door.

"What is this place?" he asked softly, not wanting to spook her but wanting to make sure she was aware of his presence.

She gave a visible start but then took a breath and turned to face him. "It was my father's workshop."

The small structure was almost completely empty now except for a wooden box and a few stray leaves that had blown in. "What kind of workshop?"

"He made shoes. He was a cobbler on an undeveloped planet before he became my mother's consort. He enjoyed the work and kept it up all his life, in private, just for something to do."

He grasped at the small detail, another piece of the puzzle that was Kyla. "How did he become her consort if he was from such a primitive planet?"

"He lived in poverty most of his life. The entire planet was barely scratching by. They got travelers occasionally, and one of them told them about Evalon. My father was incredibly handsome, and his family encouraged him to give it a try so he could send money home. He hitched a ride on a ship heading this direction, and my mother fell hard for him, the first time she saw him."

Hall couldn't imagine what the life of a consort would be like. It might be full of luxury, but it could also be like servitude—being kept for only one purpose. It definitely wasn't for him. "Did he like it?"

Kyla gave a delicate little shrug. She was still staring at the empty building, as she'd been doing when he approached. "It was hard for him, I think. He was used to working, and he wasn't used to dominant women. That's why he came here to keep making shoes—it reminded him of who he really was."

"He taught you how to make shoes, then? That's why you make boots?"

"Yes." She gave him a slanting little smile. "I moved all his tools to my suite. It makes me feel connected to him."

"You miss him."

"Every day."

"And your mother?"

Her expression changed. "Yes, of course. I wasn't as close to her though. Patrice was always her favorite."

"What happened to them?" It seemed strange to Hall that, even after so many days spent with her, he still had no idea what had happened to her parents. She and Patrice were both younger than thirty. Their parents couldn't have been very old.

"They died. They caught a fever during a vacation they were taking off-world. One of those unpredictable viruses they had no immunity to. It acted too quickly for the doctors to help. They were dead by the end of the day."

"That's terrible," Hall said, shaking his head. Advances in medical technology had taken care of most Earth-born illnesses, but the farther humans spread into the universe, the more new diseases they encountered.

Kyla gave another little shrug. She'd barely met his eyes at all this afternoon. He recognized the difference and felt an irresistible urge to change it. "I was fourteen. I'd left the palace grounds that day to explore the village. I was shocked that no one had come to find me, but when I returned I discovered why." She let out a long breath. "I haven't left the palace grounds unaccompanied since."

"It wasn't your fault," he murmured, forgetting his own frustration in the face of the pain she was trying to hide. "You know it wasn't your fault."

"I know." Her voice was very small. "But what you know doesn't always change how you feel."

Hall knew that to be true—very deeply.

She sighed. "My father always told me not to trust Court. He told me to never stop looking for what was real."

He suddenly understood another piece of what had made her who she was—why she was always holding back, why she'd never let herself go to enjoy the physical pleasures available to her.

Her father had taught her not to.

"I miss him," she whispered.

He made a throaty sound and reached out to her, following the instinctive need to comfort her, to make her feel better.

Before his hand could reach her arm, she jerked away from him, out of his reach.

It hurt like a blow, her obvious desire to keep away from him. "You're afraid of me," he said softly, thickly.

"I'm not."

"Yes, you are. You don't want me to touch you."

Her cheeks had been pale, but now they flushed. She still wouldn't meet his eyes. "A lot happens to me when you touch me."

"But it's not bad, is it?"

"Maybe not. But too much."

He told himself she was just afraid. He told himself she needed time. But a panic was rising inside him, the possibility that he might be losing her, that she might be slipping out of his hands. "I know it's new to you, but you don't have to be afraid of it."

"I'm afraid of a lot of things."

"The first time I saw you, you were fighting off a man who was attacking you. He was twice your size, but you brought him down anyway."

"I was afraid then too."

"But you still did what you needed to do. Who cares if you were afraid while you were doing it?"

She turned to look at him, meeting his eyes, as if she were checking to see what he was thinking.

He stepped closer to her, refraining from touching her, no matter how hard it was to hold back. "You can do something now too, even if you're afraid."

She dropped her eyes. "I don't even know what to do."

"That's because you've never believed you had the freedom to do anything. You do though. And you'll know what you want to do when you find it."

She looked back up, and they held the gaze for a silent minute. Hall's heart felt like it would pound its way out of his chest. He didn't even know what he thought might happen, but he knew there was something lingering in the air at the moment.

"What about you?" she asked, her voice no more than a rasp.

"I've already found it."

He heard the words as he said them although he couldn't believe they'd actually come out of him. He certainly hadn't intended to say anything like that.

Kyla gasped and turned away from him, showing him her shiny hair and straight back.

Heat flooded through him as he saw her reaction to his words. He felt naked. Completely vulnerable. He'd expressed his deepest feelings, and she didn't want them.

He wasn't going to make that mistake again. He'd learned long ago that you had to be careful which parts of yourself you showed to others. Kyla might be making him want that to change, but wanting didn't alter his reality. He'd been careful all this life. He could be careful now too.

As his eyes ran over her back, he felt a stirring of desire at the sight of the lush curve of her ass beneath her trousers. It was a normal reaction to a beautiful body, but he greeted it like an old friend.

Desire was familiar. It was known. It was safe.

It was a part of himself he was used to—a part he knew how to use.

"Why are you surprised?" he murmured, making sure his voice was thick and sultry. "You saw last night how much I want you, didn't you?"

Kyla gave another little gasp and turned back around. Her eyes searched his face.

"I found what I want," he said, making the nuance different this time. "Why shouldn't I try to get it?"

She took a shaky breath, her features relaxing into understanding. There might have been some disappointment underlying the expression, but it was too slight to know for sure. "I told you I'm not into sex. That kind of wanting is just physical."

He stepped closer to her, resting in the fact that he was good at this, at seduction. "What's wrong with the physical?"

She shook her head and turned away from him again, but this time he was sure it was because she was starting to respond to his hot look. He moved behind her, almost touching her.

"There's nothing wrong with the physical. It can feel good." He raised a hand and traced the line of her breasts, skimming over her curves with his palm. "I can make your body feel good."

She was panting now, and her cheeks had flushed even hotter. Her head had fallen back slightly, and her arousal was the sexiest thing he'd ever seen. His groin hardened improbably quickly as he watched her.

He kept caressing her, keeping his touches delicate and teasing and making sure to not touch her bare skin, lest he accidently open a connection between them again.

Her spine was arching slightly as her lips parted deliciously. He couldn't help but press his hips into her back, stifling a moan at the pressure on his erection.

Then she was suddenly pulling away from him, and he groaned in frustration at the loss.

"The physical is fine," Kyla said, turning to look at him, "if that's all that you're looking for. But we all seem to have forgotten that we can be more than that. We *need* more than that." She took a shaky breath. "Even you."

The words felt like a slap in the face since she'd evidently read exactly what he was doing, how he was trying to take control of the encounter. "Kyla," he began, reaching out to her, for real this time. "Wait—"

She jerked away from him, moving to the door of the building. "No. I don't know what game you're playing with me, Hall. Sometimes you seem like you're… real, but then you'll…" She shook her head hard. "I don't know what game you're playing with me, but I'm done. I'm not playing anymore."

He started after her as she left the building, but then he stopped himself.

He had no idea what he would say when he caught her.

She was right, after all. Just now, he'd been trying to turn this thing into a game—make it safe, make it familiar—when he knew very well that it wasn't.

~

Kyla woke up the next morning with a migraine.

It got bad during the night, so it was full-blown by the time she woke up. Those were always the worst, and the injection she gave herself first thing wasn't enough to completely knock the migraine out.

She spent the morning in bed, and she was still groggy with a dull throbbing behind her right eye after lunch. She got up to go to the bathroom and throw some water on her face, and she stared at her pale face in the mirror, glad that no one was around to see her like this. She felt so bad and so depressed that she just went back to bed.

She was trying to sleep—clearing her mind and willing away the throbbing pain—when she became aware of someone else in the room.

There wasn't any sound, so she wasn't sure why she'd even noticed the presence. But she could feel something, so she turned over and opened her eyes, blinking vaguely into the unlit room.

The curtains were closed, but it wasn't dark enough to hide the man who stood in the middle of her floor.

Her first reaction was faint pleasure since she immediately recognized Hall. Then his presence penetrated through the fog in her brain. She gasped and sat up abruptly. "What... what?" That was as lucid as she got at the moment.

"Sorry to scare you," he murmured, walking over toward the bed. "Are you okay?"

She could see his face more clearly now, and he looked genuinely concerned. But she didn't know if she could believe what she saw in his face. "Migraine," she mumbled, laying back down since the throbbing in her head had intensified at the abrupt motion.

"I'm sorry."

"What are you doing here?"

"I thought you were avoiding me. You didn't take a walk today."

"So you snuck into my room?" She was torn between indignation and something else—something completely inappropriate. "How did you get past the hall guard?"

He gave a half shrug. "You look like you feel terrible."

"I do." She rubbed her eyes and tried to pull herself together, cringing inwardly as she remembered how terrible she'd looked in the mirror earlier. "What are you doing here?"

"I was worried," Hall admitted, sitting down on the edge of her mattress. "After yesterday, I thought you were mad at me. I didn't know you had a migraine. I thought you were avoiding me, and I..."

"You what?"

"I wasn't going to have that."

She sighed and relaxed back against her pillow, gazing up at him. "We both know you're the kind of guy who prefers to play games. We also both know that you're hiding something. We both know you refuse to tell me the truth. Your being here and my migraine do nothing to change that."

"Maybe they do."

She just stared at him, unable to read the quiet expression on his face. His eyes never wavered from hers.

"What?" she demanded after a minute of silence.

"Can I help your migraine?" he asked, reaching out a hand.

She knew what he was asking. He'd done the same thing the first day they'd met and then pretended he hadn't done anything. She nodded mutely, unable to object, even though logically she knew she should.

He reached out for her, pulling her into a sitting position and then drawing her into his arms. She leaned against his chest as one of his hands slowly rubbed her back, moving up to the nape of her neck.

He massaged her gently, and she sighed in response. Then she gasped as she felt that inner tug, like something new, something different, was flooding through her body. It was him. It was Hall. The connection was stronger than she'd felt it before, and she could recognize his presence inside her now. It was like he was stroking inside her, transforming the pain into pleasure.

"Oh fuck," she muttered, her fingers tightening in Hall's shirt. "Oh fuck." It felt so good—so full—that her eyes blurred over and her skin broke out in perspiration. "Don't stop."

She could sense Hall breathing heavily as he kept pressing into the back of her neck. He was moving all through her, consuming her, melding with her completely. She'd never felt anything so incredible in her entire life.

Finally Hall broke the connection, moving his fingers away from her skin. He was panting like he'd just run a marathon, and his face was flushed and slightly dazed.

"I didn't want you to stop," she whimpered, fumbling to reach for the hand he'd dropped. She felt strangely empty without him inside her that way.

"I know," Hall replied hoarsely. "But it takes a lot out of me, and I'm not sure it's a good idea for me to be filled with you so completely."

"Why not?"

"Because I'll keep wanting more of you."

A different kind of pleasure filled her at the words and at the clouded pleasure and affection in his face.

She slumped back down onto the bed, her migraine completely gone and a deep satisfaction relaxing her body. "I need to lie down."

"So do I."

She nodded her permission when she recognized the question on his face. He pulled off his boots and then stretched out beside her on the bed.

They lay next to each other, both breathing heavily for a few minutes until she rolled over and nestled beside him.

He wrapped his arm around her, holding her against him.

"Are you going to tell me what you are? I mean, what you can do."

"You just felt what I can do."

"But how do you do that?"

"I don't know. I was born that way."

"You're more than just a Reader."

"Yeah."

"You... you can make people feel a certain way?"

"I can change how they're feeling—sense it and then turn it around. But there's no name for me. Not yet anyway."

"And no one knows?"

"Very few. My partner Lenna knows. And a couple of... of friends. But I keep it secret, for obvious reasons."

"The Coalition would want to use you." The truth was becoming clear to her now. It all made perfect sense. His behavior. How she'd felt around him.

"Yes. If they knew who I was and what I could do, I'd never be free."

"Well, I don't blame you for keeping it secret then."

"I wasn't really trying to hide things from you, Kyla. It's just not something I easily tell." His voice was hoarse again, but this time it sounded like earnestness rather than the response to his use of his powers.

"I understand." She felt a tightness in her gut, one that made her feel vaguely sick, even though she was still filled with relief from the passing of her migraine.

"What's the matter?" Hall asked. "Tell me what you're thinking."

"So you..." She cleared her throat. "So you made me feel the way I felt around you."

"No!" His body tightened against hers. "No. I eased your pain—today and on the first day we met. But I didn't change the way you felt otherwise."

"But the other night. When we were... at the masquerade. I felt you... I felt you inside me. You were making me feel that way. I've never felt like that before."

"I'd opened a connection. I didn't mean to, but I was so wrapped up in you that I..." He sighed. "It wasn't intentional. But I was just *feeling* you then—feeling what you were feeling. I wasn't changing how you felt. You have to believe me."

She raised her head so she could look down at his face, and she would swear by all that was holy that he wasn't lying. "You... You weren't?"

"No. I wouldn't do that."

"Why not?"

"I might not be the most ethical guy on the planet— on any planet—and I'll admit that I've used my gift for some dubious purposes in the past, mostly to get out of trouble caused by the jobs I do. But I wouldn't use it to get a woman into bed. That would just be rape in a different form, and I'm not one of those guys. And I'd definitely not do it to you."

"Why not me?"

"Because I want you to want me for real." He reached a hand out to stroke her cheek. It felt incredibly good, despite the fact that he hadn't opened that inner connection.

She blinked. "So what I feel for you..."

"Is real."

"You're not intensifying it or anything?"

"No."

"But it's so... so strong. I've never felt this way about anyone before."

"Good." He pulled her head down toward his so he could kiss her very lightly. "Then you might have a little taste of the way I feel about you."

She was filled with him again—differently than before. Even without that palpable connection between them, she was still overwhelmed by him, consumed by him. His strength, his spirit, the sincerity in his eyes, the warmth of his presence. She moaned softly and kissed him back, hers deeper and hungrier than his had been.

He returned the kiss, slipping his tongue into her mouth and pulling her down so her body was pressed against the length of his. His hands started to stroke up and down her body, and she moaned again into his mouth as the pleasure filled her.

"Kyla," he murmured, his lips still moving against hers. "I don't want to move faster than you're comfortable with, but if you don't want this to go further right now, one or both of us should get out of this bed."

She found his arousal and rubbed herself against it, all the tedious disgust she'd felt about sex before vanished in the wake of the bone-deep hunger she felt for Hall. "I want to stay in bed."

"Are you—" He broke off the question with a thick gasp as she reached down to massage his hard cock through his pants. "Fuck, are you sure, Kyla?"

"Oh yeah."

At her words, he made a feral sound in his throat and rolled her over onto her back, moving above her with a possessiveness that thrilled her. He leaned down to kiss her hard, and she arched up into his weight as her body responded to his.

She clutched at his shirt and then his hair as he started to kiss his way down her body, over her thin gown. She wriggled and panted as he skillfully teased and caressed her, the fabric between him and her skin only intensifying her frustration. Finally she bunched up her skirt and pulled her gown up over her head, tossing it over the side of her bed.

Hall gazed hotly down at her naked body.

"Hall," she whimpered, arching up and trying to pull him down by the shoulders. "Stop staring and do something."

"You are so gorgeous," he murmured.

"No, I'm not."

"Yes, you are." He brushed his lips down her throat, pausing on her throbbing pulse.

"You're just deluded because you like me."

He gave a grunt of amusement as he mouthed one of her breasts. "This far exceeds *like*."

"Oh." She flushed with pleasure—more emotional than physical for the moment. "But my point still stands," she managed to say after a little gasp when he tweaked her nipple with his teeth. "You're deluded about my appearance."

"No, I'm not. I thought you were gorgeous the first time I saw you, like a...." He trailed off as he fondled her breasts, making her moan and shake. "Like a violet, perfect and delicate and hidden among the plain grass."

He really seemed to believe it. He believed she was beautiful, desirable, everything she'd always known herself not to be.

In his eyes it felt like she was.

She parted her thighs as he trailed more kisses down her body, mouthing her belly and cupping her ass. She was hot and wet and throbbing for him now and cried out loudly when he moved his face between her legs, nuzzling gently until she opened for him.

He used his tongue and teeth to tease her, working her up until the pleasure was tightly coiled inside her. He flicked at her clit with his tongue and then slid two fingers into her wet pussy, stroking her internally until she was shaking helplessly.

"Are you going to come for me now?" he asked hoarsely.

She clutched at the bedding and tried not to squeeze her thighs around his head. "Yes, oh yes. Hall, please."

She sounded helpless, but she felt that way too. She'd never known she could be so out of control.

He sucked at her clit and fucked her with his fingers until the tension broke with intense waves of pleasure. She cried out shamelessly as she came hard all around him, and in the midst of it she felt a familiar inner tug, opening up a different, deeper connection with him.

Then he was with her in the pleasure. She could feel him there. She was almost sobbing as the climax continued, vaguely aware that he was choking out a helpless exclamation as well.

When she finally came down, she was fisting her hands in his hair, holding his face in place at her pussy.

He was shaking too, and he was deeply flushed when he raised his head to meet her eyes.

"What happened?" she asked, her voice cracking. She was limp with the aftermath of pleasure and a kind of release she'd never felt before.

"I connected with you," he explained thickly, raising himself up but only to collapse beside her on the bed. He was breathing even more heavily than she was. "Accidentally. I totally lost it."

She peered at him as her mind finally started to work again. She gasped. "Did you come too?"

He made a face. "Let's not tell anyone that happened."

She burst out in giggles, both amused and deeply affected by the way he'd lost control. "You came in your pants?"

"Let's not dwell on it," he muttered ruefully. "It was only because I was feeling what you were feeling. It's a lot of pleasure to handle, you know."

She was still giggling as she wrapped an arm around, nestling against him. "So you're saying you think I enjoyed it?"

His smile changed from ironic to something deep and almost tender. "I know you did. I did too. And maybe next time we can go even further. I just need a few minutes to recover."

"Me too," she admitted, pleased when he wrapped an arm around her again, holding her in an embrace.

They lay in sated silence for a few minutes until Kyla admitted softly, "I always thought I didn't like sex."

"That's because you never really knew what it was about before."

"What do you mean?"

"All you knew was the physical," he murmured, stroking her hair. "All that you saw every night in Court. To tell you the truth, most of the sex I've had in my life hasn't been much better or deeper than that. I never knew how good it could be when it's... it's real."

She adjusted so she could see his face, and she smiled at the expression in his eyes. "Yeah. Yeah, I guess so. I guess that's the difference."

They gazed at each other for a minute before she lay her head back down on his chest.

He idly rubbed her hair, her back, until he said, as if simply following the line of his thoughts, "You know, I was in prison last year."

"What?" Her whole body stiffened in surprise.

"Lenna and I were on a job. She got away, but I was caught."

"And they imprisoned you?"

"Yeah. One of those hellish prison planets. That's when I came close to killing myself, like I mentioned to you before."

"But how are you out now and still alive? I thought no one came out of those."

"They don't, usually. I managed to escape with... with some friends."

She noticed his hesitance over the word friends. "You made friends there?"

"I guess. I mean, we worked together to get out. I like them. I... think they think of me as a friend."

"What was the prison like?"

"It was hell. Humans turned into animals. If I hadn't had my... my gift, I would have been ripped apart there. It doesn't matter how clever you are in a place like that. It's only brute strength that comes out on top. I'm incredibly lucky that my gift was able to protect me."

Kyla gulped at the thought of what could have happened to Hall in such a place. "That's awful. How long were you inside?"

"Just several weeks. That was enough. I... was changed when I came out. I used to think that life was just a game, but I can't really do it anymore. I wonder if that's why..."

"That's why what?"

"I was ready to meet you."

The words were careful enough, but Kyla couldn't help but understand the implications. She shivered in pleasure that he was saying something she desperately wanted him to be saying.

"Anyway," Hall went on after clearing his throat. "I only brought it up because my friends inside there were a couple—they'd only met in prison, but they'd fallen in love with each other. And watching them…"

"Have sex?"

He chuckled. "No, although they did seem to have a lot of sex. But what I mean is that watching them together— do something as human as love each other—was one of the only reasons I was able to survive. I'd never really understood it before, but I wanted to experience it myself. And now I think I have." He smiled at her as she raised her head.

"Oh." She was suddenly terrified that things had gone too far, she'd opened herself up too much, when nothing had really changed about their situation.

The hand that had been stroking her grew still. "You're scared. I told you that when people got to know me for real, they were always afraid of me."

"No! No, it's not that. I'm not afraid of you because of *that*, because of your gift. I was at first, but not now. I was actually thinking about it, and I think I'm not afraid of it because you… You've been giving with it, not just taking."

He grew very still. "Have I?"

"Yes." She smiled up at his face. "Maybe you don't even know it. But I can feel you through the connection. You're not just reading me. You're giving me *you*. I can't be afraid of that."

"I… guess. I never knew I could actually give with it before." He was stilted, confused, but then he sounded normal again when he asked, "If you're not afraid because of that, why are you afraid?"

"Well," she began, swallowing hard, "you're still a Potential, and I'm still just a younger daughter of the royal family of Evalon. Things are pretty hopeless between us."

"They don't have to be."

"What do you mean?"

"Leave with me. Come with me when I leave."

She sucked in a breath and sat up quickly, pushing her hair back from her face as she stared down at him. "What?"

"You heard me." His eyes never left her face.

"I can't leave."

"Why not?"

"I'm not allowed. I'm the backup for the Lady Governor."

He shook his head. "You don't have to be. You can be someone for yourself."

Her head was spinning now, for a different reason than before. "But I can't leave. I belong here."

"Only because that's all you've ever known. You can't tell me you love it here. I simply won't believe it."

"That's not the point. It's who I am."

"It's who you always thought you were, but that's not all you can ever be. Come with me. Be someone else."

She felt almost sick from the fluttering in her belly. "And what? Follow you around while you smuggle?"

He frowned. "No. We can do something else. Just tell me what you want to do, who you want to be, and I'll help you get there. I just want to be with you, whatever that looks like."

She stared at him, panting as she tried to wrap her mind around what he was saying. "You're serious?"

He sat up too, taking her face in both his hands. "Dead serious, Kyla."

"But you don't like shackles, and I don't want you to feel like... like you're stuck with me just because I left everything for you."

"So there won't be any shackles on either side. No ties and no commitments. I don't want you to feel beholden to me because I helped you get out. So we'll agree to no shackles. We can be together for now, because we both want to be, and we'll let the future work itself out. I think we can do it, Kyla."

She was breathless and confused and terrified and elated—all at the same time.

Hall continued, "You don't have to decide right now, but think about it. I'll help you get away from here, no strings attached. No shackles. You can be free. You can be whoever you want to be. I know that's what you want. I've felt you inside me, remember." The corner of his mouth twitched up irrepressibly.

She couldn't help but laugh softly. "I'll think about it. It's a lot to take in. It's... life-changing. But I'll think about it."

"Good." He leaned over to kiss her gently. "I better get out of here before someone catches us. I'll see you tonight at Court."

"Hopefully, Patrice won't pick you for her partner this week."

"She won't. I've been sending her back-off vibes when she touches me." He gave her another rakish smile that made her laugh.

"That's how you've done it! I've wondered how she's been so stupid as to not choose you. You're by far the most attractive Potential there is."

"Thank you for that." He kissed her again and then stood up, straightening his clothes and pulling on his boots. "Think about it. A completely different life, away from here. It might be exactly what you've been dreaming of."

He was right. He always seemed to be right. It would be annoying if it weren't so irresistible.

She watched him slip out of the room, moving silently, and then she collapsed back against the bed.

She thought about him for a long time and then thought about her own situation.

She did want to leave. If it weren't for Patrice, she would do so without any hesitation.

But Patrice was her sister, and she'd been very foolish lately. Kyla could hardly leave her to get into trouble with the Coalition.

There must be something she could do that wouldn't mean abandoning her sister.

She mulled over it for a long time.

SIX

That evening, Kyla felt very strange as she went down for Court at the normal time.

She felt different than she had even the day before—like she'd experienced something, lived through something that no one else had.

She wasn't sure if it was how she'd been with Hall that afternoon or the way she'd been seriously considering leaving her home planet for good. Either way, she felt far apart from the people around her—even farther than she normally did.

As she took her normal seat at the end of the royal table, she scanned the room, her eyes landing intuitively on where Hall sat among the other Potentials. He was watching her, as usual, and his lips turned up just slightly when their eyes met.

She had to fight not to smile back.

He was too much—his spirit not dulling even in the strangest of circumstances. She wanted to be with him, more than she'd ever wanted to be with anyone else.

Maybe that was enough. Maybe that was the sign that she should leave with him after all.

She looked away when her confusion made her too self-conscious. Court was in full swing even though Patrice hadn't yet arrived. Established couples had already started to make out, although no one was yet going too far. They didn't yet know what mood Patrice would implement for the evening's entertainment.

Kyla wished she were sitting next to Hall. She wished she could claim him as hers. Not that she wanted to have sex with him in front of all these people, but she wished she could take him back to her room this evening.

Instead, she had to hope that his gift would be enough to keep Patrice from choosing him as a partner tonight. It would be just Kyla's luck for him to not be able to discourage her interest, and then she'd have to watch him making love to her sister.

She wondered what he would do should that happen. Then she realized she already knew. He was a practical man. He'd told her himself. He lived with no shackles—no ties or commitments. He would do whatever needed to be done to get out of a tight situation without any harm being done to him or his profit.

Whatever had happened between him and Kyla wasn't likely to change that.

It didn't matter. She wasn't expecting him to become a new man—a different man. She just needed to decide whether what they had was enough for her to leave her planet, her sister, and everything she'd known.

She sat in a daze for a few minutes, trying to figure out this mystery, until she heard a familiar fanfare from the horns signal Patrice's entrance.

The fanfare went on for longer than normal as her sister slowly entered the throne room. Kyla tried not to cringe at the elaborate introduction. No matter how many times she was warned, her sister just wouldn't learn. Calling attention to her royal pedigree was dangerous.

But a fanfare was just a fanfare. There shouldn't be anything else occurring tonight that would be too much of a problem. After all, it wasn't a royal masquerade. It was just a normal Feast Day.

Kyla was just registering this thought when Malone, the Court director, cleared his throat and gave the official introduction. Instead of his normal, "The Lady Governor, Patrice," he began a two-minute, traditional introduction, going through the entire family history and ending with "The Empress of the Five Destroyed Worlds, Lady Patrice of Evalon."

Kyla almost groaned as the crowd burst into their normal applause. Some of them were clearly thrilled at Patrice claiming back her heritage, while others were likely just going along with the majority's sentiment.

Either way, this shouldn't be happening. There might not be any Coalition officials here tonight, but there could easily be Coalition spies.

Or even just someone greedy enough to report rebellion to the Coalition in return for payment or favors.

There was no way of ensuring that a group of people this large—anywhere—would be completely loyal.

Kyla felt sick as she briefly met her sister's eyes. Patrice just raised her eyebrows and lifted her chin in a willful expression she'd used ever since they were children.

Fighting her nerves, Kyla glanced back over at Hall. His expression had sobered, as if he too knew what she was afraid of.

Kyla didn't have time to dwell on it long, though, since Patrice made her way over to the Potentials in a completely silent throne room to go through with her traditional ritual of choosing a weekly partner.

Kyla silently pleaded for her not to choose Hall.

Patrice walked past each of the men, studying them all carefully. She always did that even when she already knew who she was going to choose.

Then she reached out to touch Hall's hand, and Kyla tried not to gulp.

Almost immediately, Patrice pulled her hand back and shook her head.

Kyla let out a breath, knowing that Hall had used his gift to once again discourage Patrice from choosing him.

It was nice. Really nice. That one man in the world—in any world—didn't want Patrice over Kyla.

He only wanted *her*.

Patrice ended up choosing a dark, beefy man who'd been around for about a month. Things moved quickly after that, as the best of the food was served and more wine was passed around for the guests. The other women started to choose their partners. Kyla might have chosen Tor, just for someone to talk to, but he was on duty tonight, stationed at the main entrance of the room.

He nodded at her, and she gave him a little wave.

Since she couldn't choose Hall, Kyla just kept her seat. Better to be alone than to be forced to pretend intimacy with anyone else.

As the Court declined into its normal decadence—with people overeating, getting drunk, and coming loudly in a variety of positions around her—Kyla realized for the thousandth time that she wanted nothing to do with this.

Maybe this was her home. Maybe this kind of pleasure was in its blood. But it wasn't anything she wanted.

Better to be with Hall—even though she didn't yet fully know him—in some faraway planet than to be here, facing an endless life of empty evenings, watching people pretend to live.

Because that was what was happening here. Her father had been right, so many years ago. They were filling themselves with a pale, artificial copy of what meaningful life should really be about—like their wine that was supposed to be fine but was only a shallow reflection of the real thing.

~

Kyla didn't sleep at all that night.

She left Court feeling nauseated, and the nausea didn't dispel even after reaching her room and finally finding peace and quiet.

Her mind just wouldn't rest. She had to do something. She just wasn't entirely clear on what it was she should do.

In the morning, she decided what she really needed to do was talk to her sister. She couldn't tell her about Hall, of course, but she could at least try to talk a little sense into her.

No matter how foolish, Patrice was still her sister, and nothing was going to change that.

She asked her maid to tell her as soon as Patrice was up and available, but unfortunately Patrice always slept in very late. So Kyla had to wait four hours—until just after eleven in the morning—before she was told that Lady Patrice was awake and in her dressing chamber.

Kyla went to find her.

"You're up early," Patrice said with a little smile as Kyla entered the room. Patrice was brushing her hair, seated in front of a mirror at her dressing table.

Kyla moved a chair from against the wall closer to where her sister sat. "Early? It's almost noon."

"Who does anything before noon?"

"I do."

"Yes. You've always been a little crazy that way. I blame it on the fact that your natural instincts aren't satiated by a skillful man."

Hall was more than skillful, Kyla couldn't help but think—but then she brushed the thought away because it would just be asking for trouble if she tried to defend herself against such a trivial attack. "You promised me you wouldn't do anything to cause trouble with the Coalition."

Patrice rolled her eyes. "And what did I do?"

"You know what you did. First, at the masquerade, and then last night at Court. You know you're asking for trouble, Patrice. You *know* it."

"That's Lady Patrice to you," her sister snapped.

Kyla sighed, feeling like she'd just been slapped but also knowing from long experience that this was how Patrice always got when she felt defensive. "I'm serious about this, and you should be too. We've had it easy here—because the Coalition mostly leaves us alone. But that's not going to last forever if you keep flaunting your royal history in their face. Someone is going to tell."

"Who? Who will tell? Everyone here is loyal to me and to our traditions."

"You don't know that. It's too many people to know for sure."

"Are you going to tell?"

"Of course not! I love you! You know that."

"Then let me be who I am."

"What you're going to be is killed or imprisoned if the Coalition decides you're defying them. Why can't you understand that?" Kyla's voice broke as her frustration and helplessness grew. It was like arguing with a stone wall. Something absolutely immovable.

"So that's what you think? That we should just give up everything in fear of them?" Patrice's voice was uncharacteristically serious all of a sudden, and her eyes were

113

cold and hard. "We should give up all of who we are? Our history, our identity, the nature of our world—just because we're afraid they're going to hurt us? That's really what you think? We should let them take everything?"

"If you keep this up, they are *going* to take everything!"

As she said the words, Kyla was hit with a chilling revelation—one that changed everything.

She saw again the overindulgence and meaningless pleasure being chased by the people in the throne room last night—and she understood with frightening clarity why it had always felt so empty to her.

It *was* empty.

But they'd been left with nothing else.

She almost choked on the reality of their world—of everything that had been taken when the Five Worlds had been destroyed and then taken again when the Coalition had swallowed them up a hundred years ago, without even a fight.

"We've already lost it all," Kyla whispered, her eyes blurring with tears that surprised her. "They've already taken it all. We've just been pretending that they haven't."

Patrice stared at her, and for a moment it felt like they actually understood each other, that they shared something hard and painful in their gaze.

But then Patrice's face cleared and she shook her head. "They haven't. Not yet."

"We want to say they haven't because we're comfortable here. But we lost everything good and deep and real about this place a long time ago. No empty ritual or rootless claim to be Empress is going to change that."

"What do you know anyway?" Patrice snapped, her cheeks flushed with what Kyla recognized as real anger now.

"You've always been jealous because you can't be Empress yourself."

"I'm not jealous! Neither one of us can be Empress. And I don't want anything you have."

"You can tell yourself that all you want, and you can pretend to be worried when all you really want to do is take away what's mine. Leave me now. I don't want you anymore." Patrice's tone was regal, authoritative, ice cold.

Kyla froze for a minute in the wake of it. "I'm your sister," she whispered.

Patrice met her eyes with chilly hauteur. "I know who you are."

Kyla shook her head and turned around to walk slowly out of the room. She wasn't going to convince her sister to be smart. Her sister didn't know her at all.

There was nothing left for her here. No history, no real identity, no planet worth having. And no real family.

There was absolutely nothing keeping her here anymore.

She could make something different of herself if she left. She could be the kind of person she'd always wanted to be.

It hurt. It was terrifying. But it felt absolutely right.

She'd said to Hall once that maybe they were doing life wrong, and she realized she had been right about that. She *was* doing life wrong. She was trying to live without any risk, and that would never give her what she wanted.

She was going to leave with Hall.

On this recognition, she picked up her speed down the hall. It was too early yet for Hall to be out on a walk, but Kyla was going to go outside and wait for him. She wanted to tell him. As soon as possible. Her body thrilled with it even as her spine still shivered with fear.

She was so caught up in her decision that she didn't look where she was going, and she collided full-on with someone as she turned a corner.

"Whoa," Tor said, smiling as he reached out to stabilize her balance. "You're in a hurry."

"Not really," Kyla lied since she could hardly tell him where she was actually hurrying off too. "Just not paying attention. Sorry about that."

"It's fine." Tor glanced over her shoulder, at the hallway she'd just turned out of. "Were you visiting your sister?"

Kyla nodded, feeling glum again, despite her excitement about running away with Hall.

"No luck in talking sense into her?"

"None." Kyla let out a long breath, speaking the truth she'd come to just now in her sister's dressing room. "She's never going to see reason. She thinks it's a way of laying claim to who we really are—as a people, as a planet—and who she really is. She thinks she can find meaning in it. She's never going to stop."

"Even if it puts her—and you—in danger."

"Even if. No matter who it puts in danger."

Tor's mouth twisted. "It would be nice," he murmured, "if people would occasionally be smart."

"I haven't found that happens very often."

He chuckled softly, a little bitterly. "Me either."

Kyla waited since it looked like he was going to say something else. An expression she didn't understand twisted on his face.

Finally he murmured, "All right. So be it. We do what we can."

She nodded. "Yes. That's all we can do." She smiled at him and tried to hide her impatience. She really wanted to get outside and wait for Hall to come find her. "Are you okay?"

"Yeah. I'm just fine. I'll talk to you later." He gave a little shrug and walked away from her, continuing in the direction he'd originally been going.

Kyla gave him one last glance, and then she cleared her mind and headed for the back entrance to the palace.

The most important thing right now was to find Hall.

~

Hall went outside just after noon, far too early for Kyla to be out yet on her walk.

He knew it was foolish to feel so jittery and excited, but he did. He'd asked Kyla to leave with him yesterday, and he thought there was a pretty good chance that she'd say yes.

He didn't know for sure though. He hoped she'd have her decision made when he saw her this afternoon.

He walked down the trail they normally took, pacing back and forth from where the woods ended at the palace courtyard. Still no sign of her.

He felt like a foolish boy about to get lucky for the first time.

He still had no idea why he'd offered to take her with him yesterday. It hadn't been planned. He'd always assumed he'd have to leave her. But after connecting with her so deeply, after feeling like there was nothing more important than her, he just couldn't see himself walking away.

What could it hurt, after all? If things worked out between them, they could stay together. And if not, then nothing serious was lost. He could make sure she was taken care of. She'd be happier somewhere else than she was here.

No shackles.

No one could be genuinely happy on this godforsaken planet—all the pleasure it offered was totally fake. In reality, it was as empty as the prison planet he'd been trapped in last year. Evalon was prettier, but people here were just as desperate, stripped of what made them real.

He needed to get out of here. He was starting to feel trapped.

And he needed to get Kyla out of here too.

He paced back up the trail, trying to channel his impatience. Tomorrow he and Lenna would move their cargo, and so he could take Kyla and be out of here by tomorrow night.

Assuming everything went smoothly, and there was no reason to assume it wouldn't.

He wasn't sure what he would do if she didn't agree to run away with him. He'd have to leave her behind, but the thought was so painful he could barely wrap his mind around it.

It wasn't going to happen, he told himself. She was crazy about him. He'd tasted all her feelings for him when he opened the connection between him—all her trust and affection and attraction and understanding and need. She needed him as much as she wanted him—as much as he needed and wanted her. She wasn't going to let him walk away from her.

He was telling himself this—over and over again—when a rustling came from behind him. He whirled around and saw Kyla at the head of the trail, having just cleared the courtyard.

She was flushed and smiling at him, and his heart gave a ridiculous little leap.

When she saw him, she started to run, and he couldn't seem to move as she ran toward him, as if an excitement she couldn't control was compelling her.

He knew what was happening. He knew she was saying yes. He knew he could take her with him when he left.

He was trying to process the eruption of joy in his chest when she reached him, the momentum of her run almost pushing him off his feet.

He swung her around, closing his arms around her like he'd just been given everything he ever wanted.

"So that's a yes?" he managed to murmur.

"Yes," she said, beaming up at him as he pulled her into an embrace. "Yes, yes, yes."

He hugged her tightly, and then he kissed her, and he was so excited that he let the connection between them open just a little so he could taste her, read all her intense feelings.

One day he was going to get better about that around her, but right now he couldn't quite control it all the way.

He read her joy and her excitement and the deep faith and affection she had for him, and he wanted to swallow it, swim in it.

Beneath it he felt a little loss, a little pain, and he didn't quite understand it.

He didn't want to understand it. It put a damper on his mood. So he kissed her again until those underlying notes were buried in her pleasure and fond feelings.

He was going to take her away with him. They'd have each other. That would be enough.

SEVEN

Kyla was convinced there was nothing in the universe that felt better than kissing Hall.

Of course, she'd never kissed any other man—not for real anyway—but that didn't negate her conclusion. It didn't only feel good to her senses. Her entire being was involved in the kiss. And all of it—all of her—felt so incredibly good that she couldn't bring herself to stop.

A small part of her mind recognized that, although they might be hidden by the woods, they weren't all that far from the palace. But it was still a long time before she could mumble against his mouth, "We better stop."

Hall was really into the kiss. Even if she hadn't felt him in her mind on and off during the kiss, she would have been able to see it in his body. He was slightly flushed and damp with perspiration, and his entire body was tight, including the erection she recognized in the bulge of his pants. He groaned and kissed her again.

When she was about to completely lose control of her responses, she gave him a little push to make herself stop the kiss.

Relief washed over her in a strangely intense wave, like she'd just been trapped and now she was free. She blinked, trying to dispel the sensation and concentrate on what was more important. "We should move away from here," she said, glancing through the trees at the glimpses of the courtyard she could still see.

Then she turned back to Hall, and her eyes widened at the dazed, dumbfounded expression on his face. "What's the matter?"

He'd been staring at a blank spot in the air, but now he managed to focus on her face. "You pushed me out," he said slowly, hoarsely.

"I'm sorry." She was frowning now too since his reaction was so inappropriate for the situation. "I just gave you a little push. I was too into the kiss, and it was the only way to get myself to stop. I knew you'd stop if I asked you to. I just didn't trust myself to ask. It wasn't that hard, was it?"

His forehead wrinkled into horizontal lines. "No. I mean, you pushed me *out*."

She suddenly realized what he was talking about and why he was reacting the way he was. He'd been filling her completely as they were kissing. She'd assumed he'd withdrawn when she ended their physical proximity, but thinking back she recognized that she'd ended their internal connection before she'd actually separated their bodies. "Oh. Oh! I didn't think I could do that."

"Me either. I didn't think *anyone* could do that." He squeezed his forehead between his fingers and thumb, like he was getting a headache. "How did you do it?"

"I don't know. I just pushed. I'm sorry." He looked so shocked and dizzy that she was worried. She stepped over and put a hand on his chest. "Did it hurt or something?"

"No. It was just..." He cleared his throat. "I've just never felt it before. I had no idea people could hold me back. It's... it's... I'm glad."

"You are?"

"Yeah. Believe it or not, it's a little unnerving to have this weapon you can't always control—particularly when it could be used against people you... you care about. It's nice to know you can do something about it."

She smiled as a fond shiver rushed through her. "So you care about me?"

He smiled back and shook his head. "Uh, you'd figured that out before, hadn't you?"

"Yeah." She giggled but then remembered why she'd pushed him out to begin with. "But seriously, we should move away from here. It's entirely possible someone could pass by and see us, and then we'd be in big trouble."

Hall nodded and reached for her hand as they walked down the trail, deeper into the woods. Kyla breathed deeply of the woodsy smell of dirt and trees, trying to unravel the tangle of thoughts and feelings in her mind. She was on the edge of something here. They both were. But there were a lot of complications—including some potential life-or-death ones—so they needed to act wisely and not just get caught up in the moment, like two teenagers experiencing attraction for the first time.

She did really like that Hall was holding her hand though. It was simple. Almost sweet. As if there could be something pure about their coming together—something different from the jaded, complicated worlds in which they lived.

After a few minutes, they were far enough into the woods to be fairly safe from any discovery. It was darker here, the artificial sunlight shaded by the thick covering of trees. She couldn't see the small nuances of Hall's expression as well as she normally could.

He released her hand and said, "All right. Business first. Lenna and I are finishing up our job tomorrow, so we were planning to leave tomorrow night."

"That soon?" She swallowed, her mind flashing briefly to Patrice. "Okay. Good."

"That's all right, isn't it? It's dangerous for us here, and we need to get away."

"Of course. I'm ready anytime." She smiled at him, letting go of the threads still tying her to this planet, to her sister. Patrice had made it very clear that there was nothing real to keep her here.

Hall tilted his head, peering down at her face. "I know it's not going to be easy," he murmured.

"I'm a little sad—at leaving my home. But I've never been really happy here—especially since my father died. You know that as well as I do."

"I do." He reached up to cup her face with his hand. He hadn't opened a connection between them, but it almost felt like there was one open anyway, all the time. "We'll find another home, a place where we can both be really free."

She gave him a wobbly smile. "That sounds like heaven, but it might be kind of hard to find. Freedom doesn't really exist in Coalition space."

"It does if we find somewhere off the grid, on the uncivilized edges of their control, a planet that offers the Coalition nothing." He glanced away briefly. "You know, that couple I was in prison with. They live on a backward planet that has only one small city on it. The Coalition doesn't even have a station there. It's nothing but farms and villages and open country. I would never have been able to find them, but they reached out to me several months ago—just to see how I was doing—and I went to visit them. At first I thought they were crazy to move there, but now I can actually see the appeal."

"That sounds amazing." She couldn't even imagine a world like that, without the Coalition hovering behind every shadow, ready to strangle the life out of you. Then she giggled and gave him a little punch. "But you're not planning to work on a farm, are you?"

Hall laughed too. "Uh, no. That's probably not a good fit." He sighed, his expression changing. "I have no idea what I should do."

"Then we're in the same boat." She leaned her head against his shoulder briefly. "I have no idea either."

After a moment, he cleared his throat and straightened up. "Okay. We can figure that out later. Right now the first step is to get off this planet."

"So what is the plan?"

"There's a shipment of fresh produce arriving tonight, which means the empty trailers will be leaving after it's delivered. We're getting the wool onto those trailers. We've bribed the driver, so he'll make a quick stop at the launch port before docking his transport."

"That sounds easy enough."

"It should be. It took a while for our guy here to filter off enough wool for the shipment without being noticed, and then Lenna had to find the right driver to bribe. It's never a sure thing, because people make mistakes and occasionally turn on you. But I don't think this job should be very high risk. If you can get outside tomorrow night, I can just pick you up on our way out."

Kyla was breathing faster now, excitement and fear both mixed together in her chest. "Yes. I'm sure I can. I used to sometimes sneak out for moonlit walks."

"Meeting a secret love?" His eyebrows arched, but there was warm amusement in his eyes.

"I never had a secret love."

He gave her a quick kiss. "You do now."

She was so full of emotion that she wrapped her arms around his neck and deepened the kiss.

"So that concludes our business?" he murmured against her lips.

She was smiling as she kissed him. "Absolutely."

They kissed—deeply, urgently—for a while until Kyla's whole body was humming, and she could feel that Hall was aroused again against her.

"You know, we've never actually had sex yet." One of his hands was tangled in her hair, and the other was cupping her ass.

"We've had sex." She rubbed herself against him shamelessly. "We've just not made it to intercourse yet."

"No time like the present."

He was breathless. So was she.

"The woods don't really lend themselves to comfortable intercourse." She cringed as she pulled away from him enough to glance down at the ground, which was hard dirt, tree roots, and dropped branches and other prickly tree flotsam.

"Yeah." He groaned as he pulled away from her lips, settling her body against his in a half hug. "Maybe you should get another migraine this afternoon so you can take to your bed."

"That's an idea, but do you really think we should risk getting caught this close to running away. We were lucky no one came in and caught us yesterday. My sister doesn't always knock."

Hall groaned again. "Yeah." He'd been idly stroking her bottom, but now he slid his hand higher, up to her back. "What's another day or two? I've already been waiting for you forever. I've got to meet Lenna in not too long anyway, so we probably wouldn't have time. I never knew being in a real relationship would be such torture."

"Torture, is it?" She was aroused and rather frustrated but not nearly as much as Hall seemed to be. It wasn't just his hard cock. His whole body was so tight he was almost shaking.

She wanted to take care of him. In every way. And she suddenly realized how she could.

She gave him a different sort of smile as she kissed him again.

He took her face in both of his hands, trying to pull her away even as he kissed her back. "I love that expression you're wearing, but we better not do this anymore, or I'll be taking you against this tree—and you'd have to resign yourself to a back scratched up by tree bark."

She chuckled as she kissed his jaw, his throat, his shoulder.

"I'm serious, Kyla." His voice was hoarse and faint. "You have no idea how much you turn me on. I'm not used to denying myself, so I shouldn't tempt fate."

"There's no tempting going on here." She had the strangest feeling of possessiveness as she reached down to massage his arousal through the thick fabric of his trousers.

He grunted and closed his eyes. "Uh, there's definitely tempting going on."

"Well, maybe." She had to look down to unfasten his trousers and then pushed them down to free his cock. "But tempting to a purpose."

His body jerked visibly as she lowered herself to crouch down so her mouth was on the level of his groin. He stared down at her—hotly, dazedly.

She'd never felt anything as thrilling in life as that particular look on his face. She smiled.

"Fuck, Kyla," Hall rasped, moving his hands to her hair. "You don't have to... You shouldn't..." He gasped helplessly as she took his erection in her hands and gave the head a little lick with her tongue. "Oh fuck!"

She was torn between hot need and fond amusement as she teased him a little bit before taking him full in her mouth. She'd never done this before, but she'd seen it often enough, and she'd never expected it would feel like this. Not just about sex, but about being with him, taking care of him, giving him what he needed.

Hall seemed to be completely overwhelmed. He'd fisted his hands in her hair now and pressed his back against the tree trunk, spreading his legs slightly to stay on his feet as she started to suck.

She was a little confused when she took more of him in her mouth, and for a moment she couldn't find a comfortable way to position her mouth. But with a few adjustments she managed to get a rhythm going that didn't choke her.

Hall definitely appeared to be enjoying it. He was groaning helplessly now and rocking his hips very slightly into her mouth. She'd never seen him so out of control, and it was absolutely thrilling.

Her thighs burned from crouching the way she was, but she ignored it. She didn't think this would take long anyway. He was already pretty far gone.

She had to hold on to his hip to balance herself, but she used the other hand to find and squeeze his balls. He let out an uninhibited exclamation as she sucked and squeezed in unison.

Then his body broke in an eruption of shakes and spasms, and he was shouting out something helpless and wordless as he released into her mouth.

She coughed a little on his ejaculate, but it was a minor disruption of what had felt absolutely incredible. She hadn't come, but this was almost better. She'd never believed herself capable of being with a man like this before.

Being with anyone.

"Fuck, oh fuck," Hall was muttering over and over again as his body finally relaxed.

Kyla tried to stand up, but her legs were shaking and painful from squatting for so long. She whimpered as she clutched at his thighs for support. "Ugh. Help me up."

"Help you up?" Hall's voice was thick and fond. He reached down to pull her to her feet. "I might just fall down. Then we'll both end up in the dirt."

He didn't fall down. Neither of them did. When she was standing again, he pulled her into a tight hug. "Thank you," he murmured against her hair. "You did not need to do that."

"I know. I wanted to." She couldn't stop smiling as she pulled out of the hug.

"You want me to do you n—"

"No. I'm not really excited about the tree bark or the dirt."

"Tell me about it. My back is definitely scratched up now." He didn't look at all concerned about the fact. "But I'm sure we could figure out a way to—"

"No, no. I don't really want to. I just wanted to do that for you."

He kissed her. "Later then."

"Later." She cleared her throat. "Don't you need to meet Lenna anyway?"

"Yeah. Pretty soon. Actually, you should probably come with me."

"Really?"

"Lenna isn't big on trust, and she's not going to let me take someone else along unless she's met you first. I should have thought of that before." He frowned, as if recognizing a problem he hadn't thought of before.

"Oh. Okay. Where are you meeting her?"

"There's a little café—it's just over—"

"I know where it is. So we'll have to climb the wall?" She felt a familiar shiver of reluctance. It had been a long time since she'd dared to climb the wall.

"Don't you want to? If you're going to leave with me, you should probably be willing to break a few rules."

"I am. It's fine." She gave him a little smile. "Let's go then."

They walked quickly to the corner of the property with the vine-covered wall. Hall stopped there and studied her closely. "You ready for this? You're sure about going with me, aren't you?"

"Of course I am." She was sure—but that didn't mean it was easy. To distract herself from her worries, she gave Hall a once-over. He was rumpled and flushed and not really pulled together. "Speaking of being ready, you should probably make yourself more presentable for going out in public."

"What's the matter?" he asked.

She smoothed down his shirt and refastened his trousers. "You look a little worse for wear." She looked at the back of his shirt and cringed as she tried to brush off the dirt there.

He shook himself off and re-tucked in his shirt. Then he pushed a hand through his tousled hair. "There. How am I?"

"You still have some dirt on your back." She giggled as she looked at his face. "Plus you look like you just had sex. Try not to look so relaxed and happy."

"Not much chance of that." He gave her a kiss. "I'll live with the world knowing I just had great sex. You ready to go over the wall?"

Kyla took a deep breath and let it out. "I'm ready."

~

Fifteen minutes later, Hall put a hand on Kyla's back as they stepped into the outdoor café where he'd arranged to meet with Lenna.

Lenna was not going to be pleased.

He was prepared for it though, so he wasn't surprised or particularly worried when he saw her frowning as he and Kyla approached her table.

"What's going on?" Lenna demanded softly, glaring at him after giving Kyla a quick look.

"This is Kyla," he said calmly, nodding at Kyla to indicate she should sit down.

She was worried—glancing nervously between him and Lenna. He needed to make sure he didn't let Lenna scare her off.

"I know who she is," Lenna said, her blue eyes shooting out sparks. "What is she doing here?"

"She's coming with us."

Hall couldn't believe he was actually saying that to his partner. He couldn't believe it was true. He couldn't believe that nothing else had ever felt so right in his life.

What the hell had happened to him on this planet?"

Lenna's sharp eyes studied him closely, and she obviously saw everything she needed to see in his expression.

She let out a breath. "You have got to be kidding me." She shook her head and appeared more annoyed than genuinely angry. "Damn it, Hall. I thought you were immune to losing your heart."

He managed not to flinch although he was a little taken aback about her saying something like that. He hadn't lost his heart. He hadn't lost anything.

He was still himself—and completely in control of this.

"It's not like that," Kyla said softly. "We've made no commitments or anything. And I promise I won't cause any trouble or get in your way."

Lenna was still shaking her head. "That's nice of you to say, but how do you know it's true?" She looked back at Hall. "She's part of the royal family. Are we going to have Evalonian guards chasing us down?"

Hall glanced over to Kyla for an answer.

She shook her head. "Not after we're off-planet. They don't leave the planet unless forced to by the Coalition."

"Well, that's something, I guess." Lenna sighed. "Fine. As long as we keep to our original schedule, you can come along." Her eyes narrowed. "But there's not going to be any fucking on my ship, and I'm not going to listen to any sappy declarations of feelings."

Hall felt an uncomfortable twisting of his gut that was entirely inappropriate, but Kyla actually laughed. "It's a deal."

Lenna smiled at Kyla, but her expression changed when she turned to Hall. "You have to agree to it too."

"Of course I agree."

Lenna didn't look like she believed him.

EIGHT

Kyla woke up the next morning hoping she wasn't going to get a migraine.

It was a familiar feeling. She thought the same thing every morning as she opened her eyes. She'd close them again and mentally check her condition, making sure she didn't feel parched and there wasn't any sort of faint throbbing behind her right eye.

This morning, she experienced a familiar relief that her head seemed to be clear. Then she remembered what day it was.

She was leaving today. With Hall.

Nothing would be the same after this evening.

She hoped she was doing the right thing. It felt like the right thing, but sometimes feelings led one astray. There was nothing for her here though. She'd never get to be anyone other than a younger sister.

She wanted to be a sister, but she also wanted to be a lot more.

She just didn't know what yet.

Kyla lay in bed for a long time, trying to imagine where she'd be when she woke up tomorrow. She couldn't picture it. Only twice in her life had she been off-planet, and both had been when she'd been a child and her parents had still been alive. Things had been a little looser with the Coalition then. They'd been able to go on vacation without worrying that the throne wouldn't be gone when they returned.

She almost wished she was a child again, when the universe had still felt *free*.

Finally she made herself get up, bathe, dress, and eat breakfast. She did all of it slowly, but when she was done it was still far too early to go see her sister.

She couldn't say good-bye, but she had to at least see her today. It would probably be the last time she ever would.

To kill time until her sister woke up, she sat out on her terrace and looked out at the lush gardens and orchards of Evalon. They were manufactured to look and smell exactly as they did, but that didn't mean they weren't beautiful.

Other planets wouldn't be nearly so beautiful.

Or maybe they would.

She sat in a daze until her maid came to tell her that her sister was now up and dressing. Kyla stood up and shook herself off, calming herself until her expression was bland and natural.

Then she walked down the hall to her sister's suite.

As she'd been yesterday, Patrice was seated at her dressing table, brushing her hair. "Two mornings in a row," she said in a lazy drawl. "What have I done to deserve this?"

"Nothing," Kyla said, fighting back a shiver of anxiety. "I just wanted to see you, and this is the best time to catch you alone. I feel like we haven't talked much lately."

"That's because all you want to do is nag."

Kyla nodded at her sister's significant glare. "I know. I'm just worried. But I'm not here to nag today. I promise."

"Good. Because I'm honestly not in the mood." Patrice turned her head, her eyes running up and down Kyla's body as she pulled a chair closer to sit down. "You look different. Have you finally had sex?"

"What? No! Of course not." Kyla kept her eyes wide and innocent, although she was startled and dismayed by her sister's perceptiveness.

Patrice might be blind to a lot of things, but she'd always been astute about sex.

"Are you sure? You look… I don't know. There's a man though, isn't there?"

"Of course there's not a man."

"Don't lie to me. I know better. Oh, it's Tor, isn't it?"

"No! It's not Tor. We're just friends!"

Patrice's eyebrows drew together as she continued brushing her hair. "He would be a fine choice for a lover, but don't get any ideas about a lifetime partner. You can't have one, you know."

"I know. Tor isn't my lover!"

"It's not a stable boy or a gardener, is it? That wouldn't be appropriate at all. Someone you've seen in Court?"

"It's no one! Would you stop?" Kyla hadn't expected the conversation to go like this at all today, and she was rattled by how close Patrice was getting to the truth. "I'm lover-free, as always."

Patrice chuckled. "No you're not. But you don't have to tell me if you don't want."

"Patrice," Kyla murmured, swallowing hard.

Patrice smiled, changing the mood between them. "You'll tell me later."

"Maybe. Not that there's anything to tell."

"Of course not."

Kyla smiled too, feeling a swell of affection for her sister. They hadn't always gotten along—and sometimes they fought viciously—but they were still sisters.

"I was thinking earlier," Kyla began, following the line of her thoughts, "about when we took that vacation to the beach when we were kids. Remember? On Callison III?"

"Of course I remember that. I wish we could still do vacations. But it's not safe to leave an empty throne these days."

A throne could be dangerous in other ways too, but Kyla managed to hold back the urge to say so. "I know. But that was the only time we've ever seen an ocean."

There were no oceans on Evalon—no large bodies of water of any kind.

"Those waves," Patrice murmured, evidently caught up in the memory too. "They were terrifying."

"But thrilling. I never knew water could be so powerful."

"I didn't find it all that thrilling. I was constantly having to pull you back so you didn't go too far into the waves and get pulled out."

Kyla closed her eyes. "That's what I was thinking about this morning. Do you remember what you kept saying to me when I asked you why I couldn't go out any farther? *Because I'm your sister. That's why you stay with me. Hold my hand...*"

"*That's what I'm here for,*" Patrice said very softly, her voice breaking unexpectedly on the words.

A surge of emotion rocked Kyla, so suddenly and powerfully that she literally couldn't breathe. She squeezed her eyes closed and swallowed over it until her throat finally relaxed.

When she could move again, she reached over and wrapped her arms around Patrice, giving her sister a quick, tight hug.

Patrice hugged her back before asking on a breathless laugh, "What's gotten into you this morning?"

"Nothing," Kyla said, surreptitiously wiping away a tear as she sat back into her chair. "It just feels like we've been arguing a lot lately, and I don't like to do that."

"Me either, believe it or not."

Kyla sniffed, trying to cover for the grief she still felt. She was leaving tonight. She'd never see her sister again. It hurt so much it might have stopped her from leaving if it wouldn't have hurt even more not to go.

Patrice was watching her closely now. "What's going on? What's wrong?"

Kyla was so tempted to tell her, to beg her to come with them, get away from this planet where they could both finally be free.

But Patrice didn't want to be free. She would stop Kyla from going. And she might even stop Hall and Lenna from getting away. There was no way Kyla could take the risk.

"Nothing, really," Kyla said at last. "It's probably just that time in my cycle."

"You know, there are injections you can take to avoid all those ups and downs."

"I know. But messing with my hormones gives me migraines."

"Everything gives you migraines."

Kyla stood up, knowing she needed to leave now before she gave something away. "Speaking of, I think I'm getting one now."

"Well, go take something and lie down. Maybe it will be gone in time for Court this evening."

Kyla didn't have a migraine, and she wasn't going to be in Court this evening. But she murmured, "Hopefully. Maybe I can get rid of it quickly."

Unable to stop herself, she reached over to take her sister's hand before she left. She wanted to say something, but everything she might have said would reveal too much.

Patrice met her eyes and then frowned in a slow confusion, as if still trying to figure out Kyla's mood.

Kyla made herself walk away, but she didn't release her sister's hand immediately. She held on to it, letting Patrice's palm slip out of hers as they drew part until only their fingers were touching.

It hurt like a wound when their hands finally broke apart, but Kyla kept walking away.

She went back to her room, explaining to her maid that she had a migraine and wasn't going to go out for the rest of the day.

She cried when she was finally alone. But the curtains were closed, the door was locked, and the lights were off in her room, so nobody saw.

~

Kyla spent the rest of the day in bed, partly to keep up appearances and partly because she had absolutely nothing to do.

She'd packed a small bag, but she couldn't carry much with her. She was going to have to sneak out of the palace without anyone noticing, and they'd notice if she was lugging a trunk full of her worldly possessions.

The only things she owned that hurt to leave were the boots she'd only half-finished.

In her mind, as she waited, she played out the steps to her escape this evening. She would wait until Court was fully in session, everyone caught up in food and sex and wine. Then she'd sneak down the back staircase and tell the guard she was taking a walk.

He might think it was a strange, but he wouldn't stop her. She was allowed to go wherever she wanted on the palace grounds. Then she would meet Hall at the head of the trail, where they'd arranged, and the two of them would walk toward the road that led from the main palace entrance. In the curve, before the guardhouse, they would jump on and hide with the smuggled cargo until they got to the launch port, where Lenna was waiting with the ship to fly them out of here.

A simple plan. And Hall was always able to use his gift if they were stopped or anything else went wrong.

It should work just fine, and in a few hours she would be gone, heading toward a completely different life.

She really hoped her sister wouldn't do anything stupid in Court tonight. One day she would go too far, and Kyla wouldn't be around to help her out of trouble.

She pushed that thought from her mind. She'd done what she could. If Patrice wanted to run headlong toward danger, then Kyla couldn't stop her.

She managed to hold out until it was dark outside and she could hear the Court revelries going on two floors below her. She sat up. Smoothed her hair. Put her boots on. Went to get her bag so it was just beside her.

Then she waited another hour until it was almost the appointed time. Finally she stood up, so terrified now she was breathing raggedly.

She couldn't believe it was finally time to go down and meet Hall.

It felt like someone else was doing it—using her body, leaving the suite of rooms she'd spent her entire life in, walking down the quiet hallway and then hurrying down the stairs.

She almost cried out in surprise when she nearly ran into someone coming up.

He stopped short before he plowed into her, and it took them both a minute to stabilize themselves and figure out who each other was.

It was Tor, she realized with a wave of relief. She saw the same relief on his face although she didn't understand it.

"Where are you going?" he asked. Then shook his head quickly, as if dispelling the thought. "No, it doesn't matter. I was just coming to see you."

"What?" She blinked. There was no normal situation in which Tor would ever come to her bedchambers. Something must be wrong.

"You need to get out of here," he said quickly, urgency tight on his face. "Out of the palace. Off Evalon. You need to get your sister and leave right now."

Kyla blinked again. "What?"

"The Coalition knows about your sister's... performances. There was a Coalition scout in Court tonight, and she did another one of her claims to be Empress. The scout will have already reported it. They'll be sending a squad to arrest her. And you."

"Me too?"

"You're part of the royal family. They'll need to clear the ranks completely, after what they'll call an act of treason. Neither you nor your sister are safe." He took her by the shoulders and gave her a little shake. "I'm sorry, Kyla, but you don't have time to be shocked. You have to get out of here right now. If you're arrested, you'll be sent to a prison planet or banished on a planet dump. Either way, you're not likely to survive more than a few days. Do you hear me?"

"Yes, yes." She was almost dizzy from emotion and confusion. "But won't the palace guards—"

"Try to protect you? Yes, of course. But they only have swords. It would be a massacre."

Of course it would. Kyla felt sick at the visual of their loyal guards being killed trying to protect them in a hopeless scenario. "But how do you know it was even a scout? How did the scout know to come?"

She stared up at him when he didn't answer, and she saw a very brief expression flicker on his face.

She gasped. "You told them! *You* reported her!"

"Yes! Yes, I did." He rubbed his eyes with a muffled voice. "I told you she had to stop doing that. She left me with no other choice."

"But why—"

"Because I'm the Coalition liaison! What do you think I was doing off-world for so long? They were training me. Indoctrinating me. If I didn't report it and they found out some other way, it would be a death sentence for me. What the fuck else was I supposed to do? I'm risking my life right now by even telling you."

"Okay," she gasped. "Okay. I get it." She was angry and betrayed and hurt at the same time, but she didn't have time for any of those things. Hall would be waiting for her. He was. Right now. "Patrice is still in Court, isn't she?"

"Yes. I'll make up an emergency to get her out of there. That's as much as I can do. You meet her, and the two of you get out. Hire a ship at the launch port and get away as soon as you can."

"But what about everyone else here? Will they be in trouble too?"

"Of course not. The Coalition will want to get rid of the royal blood but keep this place as a lucrative vacation spot. Everyone else will fall in line. If we don't, they'll threaten to decommission the habitation zone, and the planet will turn back into a wasteland. Do you really think anyone on this planet is going to risk such a threat over traditions that don't mean anything anymore? You and your sister are the only ones in real danger. Now go. I'll get your sister out of the throne room. I figure you have maybe an hour before they land their hop and get here from the launch port."

"Okay."

Tor raced down the stairs in the direction he'd come. He'd have to think of a really good excuse to convince Patrice to leave Court halfway through, but Kyla couldn't worry about that right now.

Hall was waiting. And she'd have to tell him... something.

She wasn't running, but she was walking fast as she left by the back door, waving at the guard, Iram, as if she were too distracted to explain her presence.

She'd barely made it into the shelter of the trees when she was grabbed by two strong hands.

"Where have you been? You scared the life out of me!" Hall's hands were tight on her upper arms, and his face was slightly damp with perspiration in the moonlight.

"I'm sorry, but there's a... a problem." She could barely speak now. She wanted so much to just go with him as they'd planned, but then Patrice would be arrested.

She'd never survive a prison planet or a planet dump. She would be dead before even a few days passed.

"What's going on?" Hall demanded.

As quickly and clearly as she could, Kyla explained what Tor had just told her. She ended with, "I can't leave her to die, Hall. I just can't."

Hall covered his eyes with his hands and groaned loudly, as if furious with the universe for sending such complications. "What choice do you have? You can get out of here now. With me. Otherwise, you're going to be arrested too. Do you know what happens in a Coalition prison? Do you want me to tell you?"

"No! I'm sorry. I know it's terrible, but I can't leave Patrice to face that. I have to go back for her."

"We don't have time. If a squad is on its way, then we're already in trouble. We have to get out of here right now."

"I can't." Kyla was close to tears now, but she knew exactly what she had to do—for the first time, without any doubts or questions.

"Kyla, please," Hall said thickly. "She's brought this on herself. She knew what she was doing, and she put you in danger too by doing it."

"I know that. I *know* that."

"But you're still going to give up your only escape route for her? You're going to give up your chance to be with me?"

Kyla was crying for real now since she saw the harsh reality on Hall's face. "I have to. I'm so sorry, but I have to go back for her. She's my sister."

"She doesn't deserve this. Kyla, she doesn't deserve this kind of loyalty and sacrifice." His tone was bitter, rather than emotional, and his face had now become tightly controlled.

He'd lived a long time—surviving in a dangerous world. He knew how to let things go when necessary.

Kyla had always known this truth about him.

"I know you didn't have much family," she rasped. "But you had parents and a grandmother I thought you loved. What kind of a family did you have if you only loved them when they deserved it? She's my sister, Hall, and I'm not going to leave her to die."

This seemed to finally get through to him. He jerked his head to the side and breathed deeply.

Kyla wiped her tears away and waited, not even breathing, although she already knew what he was going to say.

"I can't go with you. I've got to get the cargo out and meet Lenna."

"I know," she said, managing to keep her voice from breaking. "I never expected you to come with me."

"I can't risk my life—and Lenna's—for—"

"I know," Kyla interrupted. "You don't have to justify it. No ties or commitments, remember? No shackles of any kind."

It was the first time in the whole conversation when it felt like her words were just wrong.

"Damn it, Kyla," Hall muttered, his face twisting painfully. "I can't believe you're doing this. I'm tempted to just—"

"Don't you dare." She recognized the expression on his face. "Don't you dare force me to leave with you."

He blew out a breath. "I won't. But you're just being—"

"We don't have time for this. I've got to get back to Patrice. You go on."

"I'll wait at the launch port with Lenna for as long as we possibly can. If you and your sister can get there in time, we'll take you both with us."

144

She was surprised and gratified by the offer since he would be risking harboring fugitives. "You'll probably have to leave before we get there, but we'll try. Thank you." She gave him a little push. "Now go."

Hall took one step away from her, but then he reached out to take her hand and squeeze it.

She almost choked on fear and grief and an emotion more powerful than any she'd ever experienced. "Thank you," she said again, forcing the words out through a tightened throat. "For waking me up. For setting me free."

He opened the connection between them for just a moment, and she was flooded with him, filling her completely. All his own anger and sorrow and loss and appreciation and the same force of emotion she felt in herself.

"Thank you," he murmured, "for setting me free too."

He dropped her hand then and walked away, disappearing into the shadows of the woods.

Kyla turned and ran back toward the palace.

Hall knew the steps of their plan by heart. He could do them in his sleep. He had to since he was so stunned and dazed at losing Kyla—before he'd ever really had her.

He should have known not to hope for too much. The universe had never given him anything easily—and never anything nearly so good as her.

He jumped onto the back of the transport, exactly as he'd planned, and the trip to the launch port went without incident.

Everything went perfectly. No one stopped them. No inspection. No sign of Coalition officials or the royal guard.

Except he'd left Kyla behind.

He should have just put her over his shoulder and carried her away with him. Or else touched her and changed her mind about going back into the palace.

He couldn't have done that though. He wanted her with him of her own free will.

She just cared more about her sister than she did about him.

It hurt. That truth. But it was no more than he should have expected. He'd gone into this, believing himself to be free and wanting to stay that way.

He didn't feel free. He felt like he might vomit.

The feeling didn't dispel as the transport turned in to the launch port.

He froze, terrified when he saw a standard squad of soldiers disembarking from one of the gray Coalition military hops.

They didn't turn toward him or the transport. They left the port and turned down the road that led toward the palace.

They were here to arrest Kyla and her sister.

There was no way she would be able to get past them and make her way here to him.

The blood left his face, and he was seriously afraid he might faint as he dropped down to the pavement in front of Lenna's ship.

She'd lowered the cargo ramp and was walking down it, frowning and shaking her head. "That squad gave me a heart attack. I thought they were here for us."

Hall opened his mouth but couldn't speak.

Kyla was in trouble, and he'd just left her, abandoned her. He'd never considered himself a good man, but he hadn't thought he was *that*.

"What's the matter? You look sick." Lenna walked over to stand beside him. "Where's your girl?"

"She's going to be arrested," Hall managed to say. He didn't recognize his own voice.

Lenna sucked in a breath and looked in the direction the squad had disappeared in. "Damn. Talk about bad timing. *Damn*." She turned back to peer at his face. "I'm sorry. I know you fell for her hard."

Hall cleared his throat. "Yeah. I... left her."

"Well, you had to. What other choice did you have?"

Falling for her didn't come close to describing how he felt for Kyla. He couldn't believe he'd just walked away and left her alone.

She was in danger. She was in danger right now.

He'd lived his whole life trying to evade any sort of emotional shackles. He'd always assumed that was what it meant to be free.

He'd been wrong. About so many things.

About everything that mattered.

"Fuck," he breathed, knowing what he had to do.

"Oh shit, Hall," Lenna muttered, evidently watching his face closely. "Don't do it."

He straightened his shoulders and took a shuddering breath. "I'm sorry. I have to. I *have* to."

"God save me from stupid love that makes you do such stupid things." She spoke the words under her breath— like a prayer. Then she continued in her normal voice. "Okay. I'll get the cargo loaded and wait for you as long as I can. But this is my life and my ship. If you're not here in an hour, or if I see one sign of that Coalition squad, I'm going to have to take off. Without you."

"Understood." He touched her shoulder briefly. "Thanks."

"Whatever," Lenna grumbled. "You absolute idiot. Now go. Hurry up. I'm not going to wait for long."

Hall took off at a run, keeping his eyes peeled for any sort of transport he could borrow to get him to the palace more quickly.

He was running toward a dangerous situation, one where there was only a slim chance of him getting out of unscathed.

But it was the first time he could remember feeling like he was actually free.

NINE

Iram, who was still guarding the back door of the palace, was visibly startled when Kyla approached him at a run.

She had no idea how much time they had before the Coalition squad arrived to arrest her, but it wasn't going to be long. Leaving the palace and grounds without being noticed was hard enough—since she didn't want to take the chance that the guards would be slaughtered by the much more advanced weapons of the Coalition.

But even harder would be convincing Patrice to leave with her.

She had to do it though. She'd probably lost her chance to be with Hall by going back for her sister. She wasn't going to let it be in vain.

"Sorry," Kyla said, managing a self-deprecating smile. "I left so fast before I forgot something."

Iram gave her a slightly confused smile but didn't question her any further as she hurried in. She took the back stairs again since there was much less of a chance of her encountering anyone. She reached the royal wing and was about to head toward Patrice's chambers when she saw Tor ducking out of her own suite.

"There you are," he said, looking hot and sweaty and far more ruffled than he usually was. "Where have you been?" Then he shook his head. "Never mind. Your sister is in your room. She's in... quite a mood, and I thought it safer there than in her own rooms, which is where they'll look first."

"Okay. Thank you. How much time do we have?"

"I don't know. Maybe a half hour. Maybe less. Get out of here as quickly as you can. I'm going back down to the throne room so I can stall as long as possible if they arrive quicker than we think. Everyone else thinks she just went in the love tent with her evening's partner."

"Good thinking." Kyla cleared her throat. "Okay. Wish me luck."

"Good luck." He gave her a little smile. "I really am sorry that—"

"Don't apologize. Anyone else would have done the same thing." Even the man who was supposed to want her and care about her had walked away from her when she needed him the most. That was just what people did in this universe. "Thank you for helping us now."

She paused. Then stood on her tiptoes to kiss him on the cheek. "Stay safe, Tor. Be happy."

He kissed her back, murmuring, "You too." Then he took off toward the stairs again, leaving her alone in the hall.

She took a deep breath and entered her room.

"What in the name of all that's holy is going on here, Kyla?" Patrice demanded shrilly. "Tor said you were in danger."

"I am in danger," Kyla said, surprised by how natural she sounded. A higher calm had overcome her, even though her heart still raced and her blood still throbbed with fear. It was like someone else—someone smarter and braver—had taken possession of her body. "You're in danger too."

"Then call the guards." Patrice strode toward the door, but Kyla stood in front of her to stop her.

"We can't call them. They can't protect us."

"They will, or they'll die trying."

"Of course they'll die. All of them will. And we'll still be arrested. A squad of Coalition soldiers is on their way here to arrest us for treason. They'll have laser blasters. The guards' swords won't do a thing against them."

Patrice's mouth fell open. "Arrested for treason?"

"Of course for treason," Kyla snapped, scared and frustrated and unwilling to waste time in arguments. "What the hell did you think would happen when you claimed to be Empress? The guards can't protect us, and we can't let them be slaughtered trying. We either make a run for it now, or we're both going to end up in a prison planet—or worse. So shut up and let's get out of here."

Patrice had gone white, but something in Kyla's tone or words must have gotten through to her. "They're coming for sure?"

"Tor said there was a scout in Court tonight. The squad is already on its way. We need to try to get to the launch port and make it off-world. We can figure out what to do from there."

"Maybe we can raise an army and come back to take our home back," Patrice said, looking unusually fierce.

Kyla didn't try to argue with this nonsense. "Sure." She grabbed a pair of her trousers and boots and tossed them over to Patrice. "But right now put these on. We might need to run, and you won't get far wearing that."

Patrice changed clothes in record time, and they were covering themselves with cloaks when there was an unexpected knock on the door to her suite.

Kyla jerked in surprise, and Patrice gave a little squeal that might have been louder if Kyla hadn't made a silent shushing noise.

"Lady Kyla? I'm sorry to bother you." The voice was the high-pitched simper of Malone, the Court director, although it sounded much more wobbly than normal. "But

Lady Patrice is summoning your presence down in the throne room."

Kyla and Patrice looked at each other as Kyla's heart dropped painfully. "This can't be good," she whispered, almost soundlessly.

"Lady Kyla," he said again through the door. "I know you have a migraine, but I'll have to enter if you don't open the door."

"Someone must be with him," Kyla murmured, searching the room for a weapon. She had nothing. "I'm coming," she called out, loud enough to be heard.

"Thank you, my lady."

Patrice had been searching the room too, and she picked up one of Kyla's half-finished riding boots and stuffed several heavy decorative stones that had been displayed near the fireplace into the foot of the boot. She offered it silently to Kyla, who nodded.

It was heavy and would swing well. It was the best they could do at the moment.

She took a deep breath and opened the door.

The Court director stood there, and beside him was a man she'd never seen before. He was nondescript, with the bland, barren expression Kyla had seen on any number of Coalition officials.

It must be the scout, who had been in the throne room. He must be rounding up the criminals before the squad's arrival. He didn't appear to have a weapon. He wouldn't have been allowed to enter Court if he had one.

All this she took in in the time it took for her to step out into the hall. "I'm sorry," she said pitifully. "I'm very weak with the migraine. What does Lady Patrice want?" She held the boot behind her back.

The scout reached out for her. "You're to come downst—"

She swung the loaded boot as hard as she could, right at the man's head. She got in a hit so good it surprised her. The man made a hmphing sound and bent over.

She hit his head again and then again. Until he collapsed onto the ground.

As soon as he was down, Malone offered Patrice the dagger he wore—entirely for show—in his belt. It was well made and looked sharp. Patrice tucked it into her belt. Then he looked from Kyla to the boot she still held and gestured toward his head.

She understood. They had to make it look like Malone had put up a fight, or he would be in trouble when more Coalition soldiers arrived.

"Sorry," she mouthed to the man, who'd impressed her more than she'd ever expected. She swung the boot at the side of his head, and he doubled over. He wasn't knocked out, but there'd be a large bruise at least. Hopefully it would be convincing enough.

She grabbed Patrice's arm, and they ran toward the back stairs. Kyla really hoped this would be the last time she'd be going up and down them—tonight and probably ever.

She ran fast, holding the boot with one hand and the railing with the other so she didn't trip and hurt herself. Patrice followed, a little slower but faster than Kyla had expected.

"What about all our people?" Patrice asked breathlessly when they were rounding the last flight of steps. "Will they be okay?"

"Tor said they would as long as they don't try to fight the Coalition. If we're gone, they won't fight."

"Okay. Now what?" Patrice asked. They'd reached the bottom of the stairs and were facing a wall. They could turn either left or right.

"We better take the back door and go through the woods. We can always go over the wall."

They turned left and were reaching the door when Kyla started to hear a commotion. Voices. A clatter. A lot of motion of different kinds.

"They're here," Kyla said, recognizing that some of the soldiers must already be inside the palace. "Quick."

Iram was still on duty at the back door, and he was obviously nervous, trying to look around the corner to where the squad was entering the main doors.

He gave a little squeak when he saw the two women.

Kyla was about to give a quick explanation when she heard someone running up behind them. She turned and swung her boot at the same time, and it landed square in the gut of the soldier who had almost grabbed her.

He huffed and bent over, and Iram used the hilt of his sword to knock him out.

"Thank you," Patrice gasped to Iram, who looked amazed at his own daring.

"You better leave your post, or they'll guess it was you who did this," Kyla added, giving the young man a grateful touch on the arm. "Hurry."

Iram took off around the back corner of the palace as Kyla and Patrice ran toward the shelter of the woods.

"They'll be guarding the road," Kyla panted, holding on to Patrice's arm to make sure she kept up. "We'll need to go over the wall. They won't know there's a way out there."

Patrice nodded, obviously too breathless from running to say anything. She wasn't in very good shape—not nearly as good a shape as Kyla, who walked all the time.

But fear and urgency could drive you hard, and she didn't slow down until they'd almost reached the wall.

"Not much farther," Kyla said, putting a hand around her sister's waist to keep her moving. Her own lungs were burning, and her leg muscles ached, but she wasn't about to stop.

Maybe they could make it. Maybe the Coalition soldiers wouldn't know to look here. Maybe they could get into the village and make their way to the launch port.

Maybe Hall and Lenna would still be waiting to fly them to safety.

She was still clinging to these hopes when they reached the wall. She stopped Patrice before she cleared the trees and was caught by the security drones.

As soon as they left the woods and were caught by the drones' cameras, the soldiers would know where they were. They'd be here within a minute or two, assuming they were already scattered around, searching.

"We'll wait for the three drones to pass in a row," Kyla whispered. "Then we'll have almost four minutes to climb over the wall on the vines. You think you can do it?"

"Yes. I can. I will." Patrice's face was dripping with sweat, but she looked more alive than she had for a long time.

They waited, both of them panting until Kyla had counted out the drones buzzing by. As soon as the third one was out of sight, she gave Patrice a shove forward. "Now."

They both scrambled up the vines. They were thick and strong, but they had to grab on to them the right away, or they would tear. Kyla had done this before, so she knew how to do it, but Patrice's vines kept snapping, sending her back to the ground.

Kyla was halfway up when she lowered herself back down. She planted her legs on the ground and whispered, "Try to grab a few at a time." She pushed her sister up as Patrice tried to climb. This time, she did better, and Kyla kept supporting her until she'd gotten the hang of it and was halfway up the wall.

Then Kyla climbed up again herself.

They were nearing the top when she heard shouts from behind them.

Soldiers. They'd been spotted after all.

"Hurry. They're coming," Kyla gasped.

Patrice was above her now, almost reaching the top. But she grabbed a vine too quickly and it broke. She started to slip down, but Kyla grabbed for her, barely catching her before she fell. It took a moment for Patrice to get her grip again, and Kyla had wrenched her shoulder so badly her eyes burned with tears.

The shouts were closer now, and she heard the whizzing of a laser gun.

Aimed at her and Patrice. A few of the vines near them were singed, and then she felt a burning pain in her calf.

Patrice was over the wall, but Kyla almost fell, torn between the pain in her shoulder and in her calf.

She fumbled for purchase and was shocked when, instead of a vine, she felt a big, strong hand in her grip.

"I've got you," Hall said. "I'm not about to let you fall."

Kyla stared at him through blurry eyes, her heart exploding with feeling she couldn't possibly express.

Hall was leaning over the top of the wall. He had an old-fashioned gun in one hand, and he aimed it at the approaching soldiers.

It made a very loud noise, but the whizzing of the lasers stopped after he'd fired at them.

He pulled Kyla up to the top of the wall and then helped her down the other side, where her sister was waiting.

"Hall," Kyla gurgled, barely able to stand up. "You—"

"Came back for you." He was smiling at her although he was obviously still in crisis mode. "I did. Although you two were doing so well you might not have even needed my help."

"Well, we're not going to turn it down. Are you okay, Kyla?" Patrice was wiping sweat off her face, and her expression was a strange combination of excitement and worry.

"Yeah," Kyla lied. "I'm fine. Let's go."

Hall reached out to cup her cheek, opening a connection between them and then gasping when he evidently felt what she was feeling. "Liar," he whispered, transforming her pain into a delicious relief.

He didn't keep the connection open long, but it was enough for Kyla to move again even with her injuries. "We'll have to walk." Without waiting for their response, he grabbed both their arms and started them moving. "Any transport we take will just call attention to us. They'll know soon that we're over the wall, as soon as the others catch up to the guys I shot, and they'll be heading back toward the launch pad."

"They'll see us walking, won't they?"

"We can take back alleys. I scouted them all out a few weeks ago, in case things went wrong with my job. We might be okay until we get to the launch port. Then we'll have to improvise."

Kyla was barely able to process the walk to the port. She was so weak from her injuries, despite the way Hall had alleviated some of the pain. Her head was also filled with the presence of Hall and the knowledge that he'd actually returned for her, risked his life for her.

Even though they were supposed to have no commitments, no ties, no shackles.

She couldn't begin to understand what it might mean.

Patrice was surprisingly quiet, concentrating on keeping up and perhaps too scared to ask any questions.

It didn't seem like very long before the launch port was in sight although it might have been longer than Kyla had processed in her daze. Hall's arm had supported her the whole time.

"There are two soldiers at the entrance," Patrice whispered, peering out from the shadow of the building they stood behind. "And they'll see us if we try to climb the fence. What do we do?"

Hall took a breath as if assessing the possibilities.

"Can you… use your gift on them?" Kyla asked, seeing only one option left for them.

He nodded. "I'll have to try. There are other people around, so they'll see something is happening, but hopefully they're not loyal to the Coalition. Stay here until I gesture."

He stepped out into the streetlight, and Kyla almost whimpered as he walked right up to the Coalition soldiers guarding the entrance.

She told herself they weren't looking for him. They wouldn't know he was a threat.

Hopefully.

They were too far away for her to hear what was being said, but she could see when Hall reached out his hands to touch both of them at the same time.

As he did so, he jerked his head in a way she understood. "Come on," she told Patrice, grabbing her sister's hand and starting to run.

Hall was still touching the soldiers, evidently holding them in place in some kind of stasis, as she and Patrice ran past them, into the launch port.

"Last one on the left," he called out, sounding strained, muffled. Evidently, whatever he was doing to the soldiers was hard work.

Kyla and Patrice ran to the last ship on the left, and Kyla almost sobbed in relief when the passenger door swung open.

There was no one there when they climbed in, and Kyla understood why when she heard the ship's engines power up. Lenna must be at the controls, getting ready to take off.

She glanced outside and saw Hall approaching at a dead run. The two stationed soldiers were still standing in place, rubbing their faces and evidently trying to figure out what had happened, but there were more soldiers running into the port now.

They'd caught up to them after all.

But Hall was jumping into the ship, with one laser singeing his hair but nothing else. And the door was slamming shut, and Lenna was lifting the ship off the ground, almost before the door was closed.

There were no extra planetwide protections on Evalon since there wasn't any military outpost. There were no force fields or gravitational devices that could keep a ship on the ground once it had taken off.

So the soldiers were still firing on them as the ship cleared the bounds of the port, but the shots didn't even dent the tough hull.

They were in the air. They were—maybe, maybe—safe.

"Come on," Hall rasped. "We'll get tossed around down here." He guided them up a ladder and then down a short hall to the cockpit, where Lenna was whooping loudly in victory.

"Did we do it?" Kyla asked, rubbing her eyes and wincing as the pain started to reemerge from her shoulder and her calf. "Are we okay?"

"They'll follow us, won't they?" Patrice asked, taking one of the seats and buckling up.

"Sure, but they're just in a hop," Lenna was grinning, as if she were having a great time. "We'll lose them before we get out of this galaxy."

"But they can track us?" Kyla was trying very hard to keep up, but she felt like she might faint. She'd managed to sit down, but she couldn't lean back. She couldn't buckle up. She couldn't do anything.

"Do you have any idea how often Hall and I have done this sort of thing. We're prepared. We've got safeguards against being tracked. And once we're away, we can reprogram your genetic chips so they won't be able to identify you. If they end up finding you again, it won't be because of us." Lenna rolled her eyes at Hall. "And can I just say that you were way more than an hour. You're lucky I didn't take off without you and keep all the profits for myself."

Hall chuckled. "Thanks for waiting." He was watching Kyla in concern. "Here, baby," he murmured, leaning over to press a button that reclined her seat. "We've got a medical kit on board. Let me fix you up."

Kyla whimpered at the change in position, but she made herself lean back and stretch out her legs. It felt like her whole body hurt. She couldn't even remember what was wrong with it.

She sighed in relief as Hall touched her face, opening a connection that relieved the worst of the pain again. She was vaguely aware of him opening a box and doing something to her burned calf.

"Are you okay, Patrice?" Kyla mumbled, remembering that her sister was with her and had been in just as much danger.

"I'm as good as a girl who just lost her throne can be," Patrice said, sounding like her normal sharp self, which was a huge relief.

Lenna chuckled at this, and Kyla smiled, wondering if it was actually possible that they got off Evalon alive, with body and spirit intact.

All of them had done so much better than she'd ever known to expect. Maybe people didn't always descend to your lowest expectations of them.

Not even her.

Hall had bandaged her calf and injected something into her shoulder. When the ship bounced slightly as Lenna moved into a faster speed, he reached over and buckled Kyla's belt for her.

"Are you okay, Kyla?" he murmured very softly, leaning over to brush a kiss against her cheekbone. "I feel like I've lost you somewhere."

"I'm okay," she said, blinking her eyes open and smiling up at him groggily. "Thank you for coming back for us."

"For *you*."

"For me."

"I never should have walked away."

It felt like there were tears in her eyes, but that was just ridiculous. She lifted a hand to touch him, but all she managed to do was clutch at his shirt.

"Hey, now," Lenna said, glancing back at them with another eye roll. "I gave you firm instructions earlier about how I won't allow any fucking or declarations of feelings on my ship."

"No feelings being declared," Hall drawled. "Just checking on my patient."

"Liar," Lenna muttered with a clearly repressed smile.

"Wait," Patrice said, a new note in her voice. She must have been watching Hall and trying to figure things out. "You're one of my Potentials, aren't you? The one I always changed my mind about. What are you doing with Kyla?"

"We, uh, have a history," Hall said easily.

"How do have a history with Kyla? Aren't you one of mine?"

Her sister didn't sound angry or even annoyed. She sounded confused. But Kyla heard the words and roused herself enough from her daze to speak very clearly.

She said, "No, he's not. He's mine."

TEN

Twelve hours later, Kyla was feeling a lot better.

She'd slept most of the trip to the private planet owned by Hall and Lenna's client, Charlon, who was purchasing the smuggled wool. The medication Hall had injected had almost completely healed her torn shoulder. She was still rather dazed and groggy while they were shown to their rooms by their host's housekeeping drone, but after a shower and a change of clothes, she felt human again.

She knocked on Patrice's door, feeling safe and hopeful and excited for the first time in a really long time.

She really hoped Patrice was feeling the same way, but that would likely be too much to expect.

When a faint voice told her to come in, she opened the door and looked around at the expensive, elegant room. Charlon was obviously rolling in the money. He must have even more wealth and property than the royal family of Evalon had had—far more than allowed by Coalition policies. He obviously had a method of keeping his wealth off the radar, and he obviously believed that Coalition laws were nothing more than suggestions.

Kyla found her sister on the balcony.

As she stepped outside, the sound of the waterfall filled the air with a pleasant white noise. It was gorgeous, falling down a cliff right behind the house, the water continuing in a river through jagged hills and expansive plains filled with fragrant wildflowers. The landscape was engineered, just as Evalon's had been, but it was extremely well done and gave the impression of wild, untamed natural beauty.

Patrice smiled at her faintly as Kyla came to stand beside her at the rail. "We should have done a waterfall back in Evalon," she murmured. "It really is stunning."

"It was all flat there," Kyla replied. "I'm not sure how we would have managed one."

Patrice sighed, her eyes focused on the water crashing down over the rocks. "It's too late now, I guess. I wonder how everyone there is doing."

Kyla was pleased and slightly surprised that Patrice's thoughts were with the people they'd left behind. She'd always known her sister wasn't as heartless as she sometimes acted, but she'd always been rather selfish, and it was nice to know that she wasn't just thinking about herself. "Hall said he would try to get some news. It will just have to go through channels, so it might take a little while. I'm sure they're fine though. They're not going to fight a losing battle. With us gone, they'll all go along with whatever the Coalition officials say. None of them know where we are or who we left with, so they can easily get through a drug-induced interrogation without getting themselves or us into trouble."

"Yes. That's good, I guess." Patrice sighed again. Then she glanced down to the bottles Kyla held. "What's that?"

Kyla raised the bottles up to show her with a rueful smile. "Blond or brunette? Your red hair is too distinctive. You really need to change it. Even though our chips were reprogramed and even if they don't know where to look for us, there's an off chance we might be recognized. You might be, at least."

Patrice closed her eyes, and for a moment Kyla thought she would object. She'd always been very proud of her hair. "Blond, I guess." She took the bottle Kyla offered. "Who would have thought it would come to this? I'm the Empress of Evalon."

"Patrice," Kyla murmured. "You really can't say that again. You'll put all of us in danger."

"I know. I *know*. It's over." There was something tired, incredibly bittersweet in her tone. "I think I knew it was over all my life. That's why I was holding on so tightly."

"What was really beautiful about our world died before we were even born," Kyla said. "All we were given was an empty shell. We could try to fill it with something else, but there was just no way of turning it real again." She reached out to squeeze her sister's shoulder. "We'll build something else."

"Like what?"

"I don't know. Do you have any ideas about what you want to do now?"

"What I want to do?" Patrice gave a bitter huff. "I'm not good at anything except being an…" She cleared her throat. "Being in charge. I do like it here though. This place is beautiful."

"Sure, but if you stayed here, I think our old, rather sleazy host will expect something in return."

"I'm sure I could provide."

"Patrice," Kyla gasped. "Don't be ridiculous. This is your chance to be someone on your own, for yourself, rather than just a figurehead or a pretty object."

"That's not as easy as it sounds. What do *you* want to do anyway?"

"I really don't know yet. I haven't really figured out what I'm good at, what makes me happy."

"Well, you know Hall does."

Kyla felt a wave of hot self-consciousness although she didn't really know why. She stared down at her hands on the railing.

"I knew you had a man," Patrice added.

"Yeah. I'm sorry I didn't tell you. But what was I supposed to say—hey, one of your Potentials is actually a smuggler who doesn't want to be your partner at all. In fact, I'm falling for him pretty hard. You don't mind, do you?"

"I would have liked to know."

"I know. But it was an impossible situation. My hands were tied by so many things."

Patrice let out a long breath. "I guess." She slanted a look over at Kyla. "It looks serious between you two though. You're going to stay with him?"

Kyla was afraid to answer that question since she hadn't yet talked to Hall. So instead she smiled at her sister and reached out to give her a half hug. "I'm going to stay with *you*, for as long as you'll have me."

~

A little while later, she returned to her bedroom and gave a little jump when she realized there was a man sitting on her bed.

Then she relaxed and smiled when she saw it was Hall.

"Is your business concluded?" she asked, walking over to sit beside him.

He wrapped an arm around her and pulled her against his chest. "Yes." He sighed as his other arm joined the first and he held her in a hug.

She hugged him back, her heart swelling with joy but still a little nervous about assuming it was real, it would last. "Successfully?"

"Oh yes. Charlon was very pleased. He gave us quite a tip, and he offered us another job. Lenna is over the moon."

"Another job? Really?" Kyla's heart returned to its normal size abruptly, but she managed not to let her body react. "That's good then. What is it?"

"There's some no-name planet that evidently makes this rare wine made from orange grapes. They don't export it, and they don't sell it to anyone off-planet. He wants four cases."

"Wow. Since you love wine, that must be right up your alley."

Hall was smiling down at her as he pulled out of the hug. "I told Lenna she could have the job, but I'm out of the business."

"What?" Kyla blinked at him. "Why?"

Hall gave a half shrug. "I only went into that line of work because it was an easy way to make a lot of money, and the danger made me feel... I don't know... like I was free, like I was being my own person. But I want to be someone else now."

"Who do you want to be?" she asked, reaching a hand up to cup his face.

"I don't really know." He was telling the naked truth. She could see it in his expression.

It was exactly the way she felt as well—like the world had just opened up to her, her jail cell had been unlocked, but she didn't really know what to do with the freedom since it was so new and so unexpected. "I don't know either, but it's kind of exciting to finally have the chance to figure it out."

"Yeah," Hall murmured, tilting his head down to kiss her softly on the lips. "I think so too."

She sighed in pleasure at his kiss, but before she got caught up in feeling, she knew she needed to say something. So she pulled away and cleared her throat.

Hall straightened up, his brows pulling together as he searched her face.

"Uh," she began, clearing her throat again. "I did want to say something."

"What?" His presence felt tense all of a sudden.

That wasn't particularly encouraging. Maybe he thought she was going to propose marriage or something. But she pressed on since she knew it was the right thing to do. "I just wanted to say that I can't thank you enough for what you've done for me, for us. I know you weren't planning to take any risks with our relationship, and I don't blame you. The fact that you did means... means so much."

"Kyla—"

"Please let me finish. I know we want to be together right now. And, uh, being with you is the best thing I've ever known. But I want you to know that I'm not expecting... expecting too much. As far as I'm concerned, there are still no commitments between us. So if you want to move on eventually, I totally understand. I don't want us to be tied to each other by guilt or responsibility or even gratitude. You never have to worry about that, as far as I'm concerned. There are still no shackles. We can just be together... for right now."

He made a strange little huff, staring at her like she'd grown a second head. Then he opened his mouth, but no words came out.

He closed it again, but there were still no words when he opened his mouth once more.

He shook his head in a fierce little gesture and lifted his hand to cup her cheek.

The connection opened immediately, and she was suddenly flooded with him—with all his feelings and hopes and deep love for her.

There was no other way to understand the wave of emotions she was bombarded with. He loved her. Completely. Irrevocably. She knew it as surely as she knew her own name.

She gathered all her own feelings and sent them back to him through the connection, knowing he'd understand as well as she had.

He made a soft, throaty sound as his face transformed, and then he pulled her into a kiss.

The inner connection faded as he pushed her back onto the bed, kissing her deeply, hungrily, his warm weight pressing down onto hers.

"I love you, Kyla," he murmured, pulling away to brush little kisses against her cheeks, her chin. "I don't want to be with you just for right now. I want to be with you for the rest of our lives. I want to be shackled to you—and only you—forever."

She made a whimper of pure joy, wrapping her arms around him tightly. "I love you too. I want that too."

"Good. Then we're agreed." He was smiling as he lifted his head. "Do you think we could maybe have sex now?"

She giggled helplessly as she pulled him back down into a kiss.

They kissed for a long time, and she felt his erection growing against her belly, pressed between their bodies. She loved the feeling. Loved that he wanted her so much. With his entire body.

Eventually their mouths broke apart, and he pulled off her gown before he started to kiss and caress his way down her body. She shifted as desire built up inside her, as strong as the emotions in her chest.

"You are so beautiful," he murmured, teasing her tight nipple with his tongue. "I can't believe I get to do this now, whenever we want."

She gasped in pleasure, feeling like she had the goofiest smile on her face. "It is a nice perk of being together, isn't it?"

"Definitely."

He fondled and caressed her until she was biting her lower lip to keep from crying out. She couldn't hold still, and her pussy was so hot and wet it was very uncomfortable. But still Hall didn't change positions.

At one point, he rested his cheek against her belly and breathed deeply.

"What's wrong, Hall?" she asked softly. "I'm more than ready. Surely you can tell that. And it feels like you are too."

"I am," he said thickly. "It's just…"

"Just what?"

"Honestly," he said, a wry note in his voice, "I'm actually a little nervous if you can believe it."

She gasped and raised her head from the pillow. "Seriously? Why?"

He raised his head too, so their gazes met. "I don't know. This is just so… real. I know it doesn't make sense."

"It does make sense. I'm a little nervous too. But I really want to do this. Don't you?"

"Yeah." He gave an ironic huff. "I'm not sure how much longer I can wait."

"Then let's go."

He smiled at her as he pushed himself up so he could move higher up her body. She spread her legs to make room for him between them, and he kissed her deep and hard. As he did, his hand slid down to feel between her thighs, finding her wet pussy.

She gasped as he slid two fingers inside her, and then gasped again as he opened a connection and she suddenly felt a rush of *him* in her mind.

"Sorry," he gasped. "I've got to stop doing that. I just can't seem to keep control of it around you."

"You don't need to stop. I love it."

He smiled against her lips. "I'm not used to being a man who loses control like that."

"Well, start getting used to it."

He was chuckling as he kissed her, and his body shook deliciously against her. He fucked her with his fingers for a minute until she was open and pliant for him. Then he positioned his hard cock at her entrance, and she gasped as she felt the beginning of the penetration.

"You're ready?" he murmured.

"Yeah. Oh yeah."

He gently eased himself in and slid out again, only to slide in even more. It didn't hurt, but it was very tight, and she kept arching up off the bed as he moved inside her deeper and deeper.

"How is it?" he asked breathlessly, holding himself still for a moment.

She couldn't stop gasping and clutching at the bedding. "Good. It's... tight. But good."

"I promise I'll be gentle."

"Well, don't be too gentle."

He laughed again and adjusted his position so he was fully inside her. She bent up her knees around his hips and made a funny little sobbing sound.

"You're all right?" he asked. His face was damp with sweat, and his features were twisted with palpable tension.

"More than all right. Open the connection and feel for yourself."

He shook his head. "If I do it now, I'll probably come right away, and that would be very embarrassing. You have to come first."

"Okay," she panted. "You can wait a little longer then."

He leaned down to kiss her, and he kept kissing her as he began to rock his hips against hers, moving his erection inside her.

It was strange. So strange. But it also felt deep and real and raw and intimate. She loved it. She wanted even more.

She wrapped her arms around him, kissing him back and trying to move her hips in rhythm with his. It took her a minute to get it right, but eventually their motion together started to feel better and better.

She gasped in pleasure as Hall lifted his head to gaze down at her. His eyes were full of desire and heat and intensity and love. His motion accelerated, and she cried out in response to how good it felt. She tried to wrap her legs around him, wanting to feel him even more.

He grunted as the penetration deepened, and then he took her even harder. Both of them were panting now, and the bed was beginning to shake.

Pleasure had coiled tight at her center, and she desperately wanted it to release. She moved eagerly, shamelessly, trying to chase it, trying to get there with him.

"Fuck, baby," he muttered. "You feel so good. It feels like you're going to come."

"I am," she choked, her body flushing with heat. "Close. So close."

"Love you so much. So much." He panted out the words in time with his rhythm.

Her heart overflowed so intensely that the pleasure broke inside her. Her pussy clamped down around his cock, and her body started to shake helplessly.

Then suddenly she felt the connection open between them, and all her pleasure and release and emotion spilled out into him. And his feelings rushed into her. And they were together in it, the power of it so overwhelming that it blinded her momentarily.

He let out a hoarse shout as his body started to jerk. He was coming hard. She could feel it in his body, feel it inside of herself.

He collapsed on top of her as the internal connection finally broke. She couldn't move, couldn't speak, could barely breathe.

"Oh fuck," Hall muttered, over and over again.

"That was… That was… That was…" There were no words to describe it.

With effort Hall finally raised his head. "My sentiments exactly."

She giggled, still exhausted but feeling a little more like herself. She hugged him against her, and after a minute, he turned them over onto their sides, still tangled together.

"I can't believe I spent my whole life not doing that," she said after a moment.

"Me too. I've never done that before either."

"Good. I'm glad."

"So am I," he admitted, smiling at her.

He was softening inside her, and her pussy felt raw and sore. She whimpered slightly when he pulled himself out and readjusted them so she was nestled beside him.

They dozed for a while, wrapped up in each other's arms until Kyla started to get overly warm and her arm was falling asleep. Reluctantly she rolled away from Hall.

He blew out a breath beside her and stretched his arms and legs.

"Were you hot and uncomfortable too?" she asked.

The corner of his mouth tilted up. His hair was a rumpled, adorable mess. "Maybe a little. Not that I'd ever admit it."

"Of course not."

They smiled at each other until Kyla finally asked, "But seriously, what are we going to do tomorrow? Where are we going to go? We can't stay here since your business is done, and we need to go somewhere to… to regroup and figure out what's next."

"Yeah. I know. I was thinking about that. My friends— you know, from prison—I told you they live on this rustic planet on the edges of civilized space. It won't be what you and Patrice are used to, but I'm sure they'd let us stay with them for a while. There is only one Coalition outpost in the six connected star systems. It's as far away from the Coalition as we can get."

"That sounds perfect," Kyla said, rolling over to face him. "You're sure your friends won't mind?"

"I'm sure they wouldn't. We've helped each other out before. I've only seen them once since we got off that prison planet, but I think they like me."

"Great. Let's do that then."

"I've got to warn you, it's rather primitive."

"You're talking to someone who grew up on Evalon."

"Yes, but Evalon was intentionally archaic. This place is uncivilized. No replicators, no habitation generators, just raw nature."

"Sounds good to me. We could use the break to figure out what we're going to do." She reached over to stroke his face, feeling the bristles on his jaw. "Maybe you should go with Lenna after all. You're a wine expert. Maybe you could learn to be a wine merchant or something."

He made a face and shook his head. "I just want to plant myself somewhere for a while."

"Me too."

"We'll figure it out."

"I know."

"To tell you the truth," Hall said, looking like he might drift back to sleep, "I'm looking forward to not knowing exactly where I'm going."

~

Two days later, Lenna dropped them off at a barely-there launch port on a planet that felt like it was on the fringes of the known universe.

Hall waved at a man who was waiting near the entrance next to a rickety transport that looked about a hundred years old.

"Oh my," Patrice breathed, looking as lovely as ever with her newly blond hair and very uncomfortable in the undeveloped environment. "That's your friend? He looks scary."

The man they approached did look quite intimidating. He was much taller and broader in the shoulders than Hall. His hair was cropped very close, and he had strong, starkly chiseled features that weren't exactly handsome but were striking anyway. As they got closer, Kyla saw he had startling blue eyes in his dark face.

"This is Cain," Hall said, smiling and shaking the other man's hand. "Patrice and Kyla."

They both shook the man's hand. He didn't smile at them, but he nodded, which Kyla took as a welcoming expression from him.

"He's not as bad-tempered as he looks," Hall told them in a stage whisper.

Cain just gave him a grunt and a glare.

Hall did most of the talking on the ride back to Cain's place, which Kyla discovered was an old-fashioned ranch. She stared around at the herds of real cattle they passed along the unpaved road.

"Those are all yours?" she asked, turning to look at Cain with wide eyes.

He nodded, his eyes softening slightly, as if he sensed and appreciated her excitement about his ranch. "Yeah. Why?"

"Don't tell me you're a fan of cows?" Hall said with a laugh, putting his arm around her and squeezing gently.

"I was just thinking of leather. Real leather. Can you imagine the kinds of boots I could make? All I've ever used before was replicated stuff."

"You make boots?" Cain asked.

"Yes," she admitted, realizing it sounded rather silly. "Just for fun."

Cain smiled for real as he stared out at the road in front of them. "Nice."

Kyla decided that, despite his stoic nonverbal manner, Cain must be a really good guy after all.

~

At the ranch, they were met by Cain's wife, Riana.

Riana was slim and pretty—and much more smiling and openly welcoming than her husband. Kyla immediately liked her. She saw from the rings on their fingers that Cain and Riana had actually been married in an old-fashioned ceremony. Almost no one did that anymore since the Coalition frowned on it.

Kyla liked the idea of it. A real rebellion against the Coalition might be decades in coming although a few groups had tried recently and been mercilessly crushed. But there were small acts of rebellions still available to people.

A quiet, happy marriage like Cain and Riana's was one of them.

Maybe one day she and Hall could get married too.

She wasn't about to suggest it, of course—not so soon in their relationship—but it gave her hope. Possibilities still waiting for her in a future that was still unknown.

As they started toward the house, a large dog ran toward them, barking enthusiastically. He reached Patrice first and jumped up on her, panting loudly with his large tongue hanging out.

Patrice squealed—either from fear or outrage.

"Max," Cain ordered. "Down."

The dog got down immediately, sitting obediently but still shifting his rear end, as if he was hard-pressed to obey. He was still panting eagerly and looking between Patrice and Kyla.

Kyla laughed. "He seems like a very friendly fellow."

"He doesn't get many visitors," Riana explained, giving the dog a scratch behind the ears. "He didn't hurt you, did he?"

Patrice still looked rather dazed from being jumped on by the dog. She brushed at her clothes and managed a smile. "Oh no. It's fine."

Kyla tried not to laugh again—since her sister was obviously trying to be polite. She wasn't an animal person.

To make up for her sister's lack of enthusiasm, Kyla crouched down to pet the dog, who wiggled his body ecstatically. When she stood up, Hall was smiling at her, and Cain was giving her a nod.

Evidently, treating his dog well was the way to Cain's heart.

They had very little luggage, but Cain and Hall carried it in for them to a clean, pleasant house that looked simple and comfortable but without any of the luxuries they were used to.

"Wow," Patrice said, looking around.

Kyla knew what her expression meant. She'd probably never imagined that anyone could live in such a primitive way. To cover for her sister, she smiled at Riana. "I love it. Thank you so much for having us."

"Of course," Riana said with a returning smile.

Kyla aimed a discreet glare at her sister before she turned back to Riana. "It's really nice of you to have us, when we're fugitives."

Riana chuckled and wrapped an arm around Cain's waist when he came to stand beside her. "We're fugitives too. And Hall must be a fugitive about a dozen times over."

"What's that?" Hall asked, coming out of the bedroom where he'd been setting their stuff. "Did you just say a dozen times? Don't insult me. I'd say at least two dozen."

"If you keep this up, you'll have a planet full of fugitives here," Kyla said.

While the others laughed, Cain gave a soft grunt and muttered, "I could live with that."

~

That evening, the moment Kyla climbed under the covers, Hall pulled her into his arms and rolled over on top of her.

She laughed and wrapped her arms around his neck. "Well, hello to you too."

He was smiling as he kissed her. "So what do you think?" he asked as he pulled back enough for them to look at each other.

"About sex?" she asked. "I'm in."

"That's good to know since I'm going to be *in* very soon. But I meant about this place, about Cain and Riana. Will you be all right staying here for a few weeks?"

"Of course! I think they're great, and I love this ranch. Cain said he'd show me how to make leather." She could barely contain her excitement at this possibility.

"Good. Good. He really likes you."

"How can you tell? The man almost never smiles."

"That's just his way. You know it's not real, don't you? Once you get to know him—"

"Oh, I know. I could tell right away. He's a good guy, and I really like Riana. You don't have to worry about me. Now, Patrice, on the other hand…" She trailed off, torn between amusement and worry.

"I've got to say," Hall murmured, "I wouldn't have missed for the world Cain telling her to help Riana muck out the stable."

Kyla giggled, not even feeling guilty for laughing at her sister. It might do her good to see what the rest of the world was like. Patrice seemed so lost right now. Far more lost than Kyla felt. "And when he reminded her that she wasn't an empress anymore. You should have seen her expression." She sighed then. "Poor Patrice."

"She'll be fine. If she doesn't want to work, she could always hook up with a rich man. I know Charlon was interested in her. She's gorgeous. Other men will be interested too."

"Yeah, but I don't really want her to sell herself that way just so she could live comfortably. She's got a lot more to offer than that."

"I know," Hall agreed, his tone changing. "But you can't always control what other people do—even the people you love."

"Yeah." She sighed again. "I know you're right. Hopefully, she'll find her way."

Hall kissed her again, as if trying to comfort her. "I'm sure she will."

Kyla decided they had better things to do right now than talk about her sister. After all, she had a big, warm, strong, handsome man between her legs—a man who loved her and never wanted to leave her. "So you really think she's gorgeous, do you?" she teased.

Hall shook his head, his eyes very soft. "Not nearly as gorgeous as you."

"Good answer," Kyla said, right before she pulled him down into another kiss.

EPILOGUE

A month later, Kyla was on a horse—a real, Earth-pure stallion rather than the animals engineered through hormones and hybridization that she'd always known on Evalon.

She was riding at a gallop, trying to keep up with Hall's larger stallion.

They were still on Cain and Riana's ranch, and Kyla had never been happier in her life. She loved this planet, and she loved both Cain and Riana. She'd gotten to know some of the other families in the community, and she'd never before felt like she was really a part of things the way she was here.

She'd made several pairs of boots already. A few she'd given away, but the rest she'd sold—for a surprising amount of money for a community that wasn't particularly wealthy.

Plus there was Hall. She loved him most of all.

He was grinning at her over his shoulder, and he called to her, "Can't you get your nag to keep up?"

Kyla dug her ankles into the horse's side, and the stallion responded by speeding up.

She laughed out loud as she and her stallion moved up beside Hall. She felt like she was flying, like she was completely free, like nothing could hold her back.

Nothing could hold her back, except the fatigue of her horse, who eventually had to slow down.

Hall slowed his down too, and they cooled the horses off at a trot and then a walk as they reached the top of a steep hill.

"Are we almost there?" Kyla asked, breathing in wind and the fresh scent of dirt and grass.

"Yes."

"Where exactly are we going?"

Hall pulled his horse to stop, so Kyla did too. Hall nodded down the other side of the hill. "We're here."

Kyla looked at the landscape in front of them. It was beautiful, the hill sloping down toward a broad river, with fields beyond it that looked like a farm. "Why are we here?"

"Because that piece of property is for sale. You like it on this planet, don't you?"

"Of course. But that's a farm, isn't it? You don't want to be a farmer, and I don't want you to do something you don't really like just so we can stay here."

"I'm not going to be a farmer. Not really anyway. I've been doing some tests on the soil. The climate is a little colder than ideal, but I think the soil there would work for some really interesting kinds of grapes." His eyes were sparkling the way they did when he had a really good plan.

"Grapes?" She gasped when it processed in her mind. "A vineyard? You want to start a vineyard?"

"And a winery." He was watching her closely, as if checking her reaction. "I'd have to hire some help, but I could start small. I could do what my parents did. I think I would like it if that's all right with you."

She was almost choking on her joy and excitement as she realized that Hall could be happy, he could do something he wanted to do, and they could stay on this planet. She scrambled off her horse, almost stumbling when she reached the ground.

Hall was dismounting too, and he caught her and pulled her into a hug. "So that's a yes, is it?" he murmured into her hair.

"Why don't you feel for yourself?"

He pressed his mouth against her neck, opening a connection that filled them both with each other's love and joy and excitement and hope.

It was so strong it rocked her. She could barely stand up. Tears were streaming down her face when he finally broke the connection.

She was flushed and gasping as she said, "Promise me you'll never do that particular thing with anyone else."

He'd been smiling, but his expression sobered as he looked at her. "Of course I won't. You know that, don't you? It's as intimate as sex is to me now, and you're the only one I'll ever share that with."

She brushed away her tears. "Good. That's what I thought."

He shook his head and took her hand as they led the horses down the hill and tied them up so they could explore the piece of property.

"Do you have enough money stashed away to afford this place?" Kyla asked as they approached the big house that overlooked the river.

"Yes. Prices here are cheap compared to the rest of Coalition space. I've got enough. Lenna said she'd be in this general area next week, so she could pick us up and we could go collect it."

"Perfect. I'll be glad to see Lenna again. How is she doing?"

"Same as always. She told me that I might have settled down, but she's not about to cave on that."

"At least she's having a good time with it. Hopefully, she won't get in trouble with the Coalition."

"She has a way of making things work for her. I think she'll be all right."

Kyla cleared her throat. "When we're collecting your stash, if we're in the area, maybe we could stop and visit Patrice?"

"Of course we can," Hall said, brushing a hand down her hair in a silent, comforting gesture.

"I can't believe she went back to Charlon. I mean, she's basically his mistress now."

"Yeah, but it's as close to the life she knows as she can get. People don't always change that quickly."

She sighed, letting out her anxiety and disappointment with her breath. Patrice had left two weeks ago, after giving up on living a primitive life on an uncivilized world. Kyla was getting used to the idea at last. "But what happens when he gets tired of her? She won't be that beautiful forever."

"She'll have to figure it out then. She can always come and live with us. You know that, right?"

Kyla leaned over and kissed Hall's shoulder. "Yes. I know that. It means a lot since I know you don't really like her. Thank you."

"I've never been bound to anything as tightly as I'm bound to you. I'm hopelessly shackled for the rest of my life." Hall's eyes were warm and soft. "But it's the kind of bondage I've spent my life looking for. What's yours is mine. Including your sister."

"Same here," she whispered, too emotional to say anything more.

Hall gave her a little hug before he said, "All right. So do you want to look at this house? The owners let me borrow the key so we could go in."

"Yes, I want to see the house. I can't wait! I've always wanted a house of my own."

"So have I," Hall admitted. "So have I."

ABOUT THE AUTHOR

Claire has been writing romance novels since she was twelve years old. She writes contemporary romance and women's fiction with hot sex and real emotion.

She also writes romance novels under the penname Noelle Adams (noelle-adams.com). If you would like to contact Claire, please check out her website (clairekent.com) or email her at clairekent.writer@yahoo.com.

Books by Claire Kent

Revenge Saga
Sweet the Sin
Darker the Release

Escorted Series
Escorted
Breaking

Nameless Series
Nameless
Christening
Incarnate

Hold Series
Hold

Release